SO-CBA-965

EAN

ISBN 1-56333-368-6

9 781563 333682

50595

A sampler set to introduce some of the hottest
contemporary lesbian erotica.

The Best of
LINDSAY
WELSH

"These tales are extremely enjoyable...reading may be
interrupted by increased passion."
                                        —Perception

Finally the wine is finished, and we beg off, explaining that I need some sleep. We kiss them good-bye and head back down the busy street to my apartment. On the way I lean over for a quick kiss, which turns passionate very quickly. Leslie is just as much in need as I am. We duck into a narrow alleyway between two stores. Her tongue is in my mouth immediately, probing and pressing against mine as hard as she can. She takes my hand and guides it between her legs. I can feel her wetness through her shorts, and her flesh seems on fire. She moans and rubs against my hand, her fingers on my breasts through my shirt. We grope like two sex-starved people, kissing, feeling, grabbing each other with only one thing in mind. Reluctantly, I break away and take her hand, pulling her quickly along the crowded sidewalks. I can't get home fast enough, and Leslie keeps up with me.

Also by LINDSAY WELSH:

The Best of
LINDSAY
WELSH

ROSEBUD

First Rosebud Edition 1995

First Printing November 1995

ISBN 1-56333-368-6

Cover Design by Dayna Navaro

Manufactured in the United States of America
Published by Masquerade Books, Inc.
801 Second Avenue
New York, N.Y. 10017

THE BEST OF LINDSAY WELSH

INTRODUCTION

Many years ago, a friend suggested that I put my wildest sexual fantasies on paper and share them with others.

Little did I ever think that they would become popular, and I certainly never expected that one day my publisher would call me up and ask me to put my favorites into a single volume. Having other people enjoy my fancies and my experiences is a turn-on in itself.

In this age of sexually transmitted diseases, especially AIDS, there are critics who complain that books such as these are irresponsible because the characters don't always practice "safe sex." I disagree.

These are stories, fantasies, and are designed to give readers a break from everyday worries and instead, indulge themselves in hot, fast-moving, satisfying sex scenes. We don't read science fiction novels and complain because the author fuels the rocketship with helium and coffee grounds; we're just interested in what happens when the characters land on Venus. Likewise, responsible adults know that reality means caution and dental dams, but fantasies mean whatever gets you off.

Loosen your clothes (if you're wearing any), sit down, and prepare yourself for steamy women enjoying over-the-top sex. And strap yourself in. I promise it's going to be a wild ride.

—Lindsay Welsh

"PROVINCETOWN SUMMER"
(from *Provincetown Summer & Other Stories*)

The streets of Provincetown are old and the buildings hug up to them the way I curve into Leslie's body late at night. The salt of the ocean water is the taste of her skin in the lazy, hot afternoons, with the fan revolving overhead and a glass of ice and lemon by the overstuffed sofa. The grass that grows up through the sand sways as gracefully as she does when she collects shells on the beach at low tide.

I sit on the sand and watch her with a hollow feeling in my chest. Her lovely small breasts move slightly under her thin shirt as she reaches down to pick up a shell. She comes down almost every day to collect shells at low tide, then returns to her studio where she turns them into exquisite little souvenirs for the tourists who come to Cape Cod each summer. They are extremely popular, and I can see why; they are as sensuous, as windswept, as much a part of the ocean and the beach as Leslie is. I see her moods in the bright strokes of paint she adorns the fragile shells with. In the winter, she paints stunning canvases, but it is the seashell trinkets, along with an occasional spot as a waitress or grasscutter when funds get low, that pay the rent and keep the refrigerator full.

Provincetown, Massachusetts is her year-round home, which is proudly announced on the bumper sticker that is probably the only part of her car that isn't rusty, to differentiate her from the tourists and the summer people who live on the tip of the Cape only when the weather is good. I am one of these. I come here each year in the late spring, with boxes of books and my trusty typewriter, from the small trailer park in Florida that is my home base. I love Provincetown with a passion. I love its weather-beaten gray houses, its clamshell-lined driveways, and especially the fact that I can be openly lesbian and not have to hide. My downfall is the winter here, when fierce icy storms rage across the sand dunes and the temperature drops to the point where cars—and I—won't start.

I cannot tolerate the winters, which seem to rejuvenate Leslie after a summer of heat and humidity. She thrives on the cold, and basks in the tight community spirit that fills the residents left behind when the throngs of summer people pack up and leave. So each fall we say good-bye, like college lovers, and I make my way back down the coast to the palm trees and the warm December days, when I can go outside in slippers and T-shirt to pick up my morning paper. Leslie remains behind, sending letters, painting pictures. I do not know if she has lovers when I am gone; I do not ask, and she does not ask me. But each spring, when I return to the apartment over the art gallery, which I have rented for the last seven years, we are just as if the winter had never happened, as if nothing had ever torn us apart.

I look out over the sleek sand, a sight not much different than that of my other home far away. Here, though, there is more for me. Barefoot, bent over, her creamy ass tight against her shorts, Leslie makes me want to run over the hard-packed sand and take her right there, in the salty foam and seaweed. I am on a high today; the book I have been slugging away at for almost a year is only a few days from completion.

The nights are a little cooler now, though, and the streets are not as crammed with tourists as they were in July. Leslie and I are both fiercely stubborn; she will not come to Florida, for she loves the different seasons, and I cannot remain here. Instead, we choose to fill our summers with intense, frequent lovemaking, if only for a short time, and go our separate ways when the long winter is inevitable.

Most of our friends think we are totally hopeless, and in the fall when I hold her tight and my tears spill out onto her hair, I think they are right. I wonder why I can't give in and spend the winter on the ice-bound cape. But the separation becomes a breathing space for us, and in spring when I return, feeling a little foolishly like the swallows, it is as if I have never left, and we continue our summer love just as feverishly as before.

Her bag filled with shells and stones, Leslie comes back from the water's edge. We get on our bicycles and return to town. She lives on the upper floor of an old frame house a few blocks from the commercial center of the town. The smallest room is her bedroom, the next largest a combination of living room and dining nook, with a tiny kitchen off to the side. The largest room, with one wall almost completely filled with wooden-framed windows, is her studio, which is always filled with a mishmash of completed painting, works in progress, seashells, glue, paintbrushes and a photograph of me, in a silver frame, on one wall. I am moved by the prominence of my picture, but in my orderly fashion, I can never figure out how on earth she turns out anything from the mess of materials that are cluttered on the tables and floor.

Even though we are together at some time almost daily, both of us need solitude to work, and when I write or she paints we leave each other alone. Hence the need for separate apartments, although it isn't uncommon that one of them is empty throughout the night. Sleeping with her and feeling her smooth, warm body pressed against mine is one of the joys I have with her, especially when we incorporate some sex into our morning coffee routine.

We put the bicycles on the porch and I follow her upstairs, enjoying the sight of her beautiful ass above me as she walks. She leaves the bag of shells sitting on the table and puts her arms around me. We kiss slowly, and she reaches under my shirt to run her fingers around my nipple. I push my tongue into her mouth, wanting more.

I kiss her throat, the back of her neck, the sweet spot by her earlobe, her silky eyelids and brush the tip of my tongue against her temples. I love to hold her like this. Her skin is still warm from the sun and tastes slightly salty, as if all the ocean has swept over her. I reach into the back pocket of her shorts to cup her firm ass cheeks, knowing how lovely they look naked and pressed up against me. She reaches down to hold my ass and we stand for the longest time, fingers kneading firm flesh, kisses planted on anything we can reach.

Leslie moves away, smiles at me and slowly, seductively, removes her shirt. She wears no bra, and her small, firm breasts cry out for attention. I sit her down in the overstuffed chair, then kneel before her.

My tongue finds her nipples instinctively. I love to suck them in, one at a time, then run my tongue slowly around each one while it's still between my lips. I bite them gently, pulling on them, nibbling at them, still flicking my tongue over the tender tip I hold between my teeth. I run my hands up and down her slim body, over her breasts, and down to tease the spot between her legs that feels warm and salty even through her shorts. I move back up to her lips, and she takes my fingers into her mouth, sucking at them, pushing her tongue between them. It makes me weak with desire for her.

I lean back, and she reaches down to help me pull off her shorts and panties. Her pussy is a lovely, sweet oasis between blonde-haired lips, and I could stare at it all day. I trace the designs of the folds with the tip of my tongue; she sighs, and I know so well the sweet electric tinglings that must be rising from my touch.

I probe with my tongue and hands, and my finger reaches the sweet nub of flesh at the top. Leslie groans. Quickly I replace my finger with my tongue. As always, she tastes both raspberry-sweet and salty at the same time, and I lap at the moist folds eagerly. She holds my head and pushes me deeper into her. I stick my tongue as far into her hole as I can, fucking her with it. Her hands in my hair set up a rhythm and soon my tongue is sopping with her lovely juices. My face is wet and all I can smell is the perfume of her nectar. I would love to drown in her pussy if I could.

I enjoy teasing her. I move up and lash my tongue over her clit, until I can feel her tighten up, ready to come. Then I return to her hole, lapping with long strokes, and she relaxes, moaning. I go back to her clit, kissing it, sucking at it, and again when I feel her getting close I leave it, so that she collapses in the chair, nearly at the edge of orgasm. Finally, after several long minutes of teasing her cunt, I go back to her clit and center all of my attention on it, licking, flicking, lapping.

I know Leslie's responses as well as I know my own. All of her muscles tighten, and even her toes curl up. She pushes her pussy against my face, rubbing herself on the tip of my tongue. My tongue and her sweet clit are one. When she comes, she is very vocal, crying out, pushing me into her, shaking. My own cunt is throbbing as I lick every last quiver out of her. I know exactly how good it felt.

Although she is still gasping for breath, she is on me in a moment, opening my shirt to reach my sex-swollen breasts. She knows how much I love to have them touched, and she leads me into the bedroom so that I can lie down. She takes forever on my tits. She kneads them, kisses them, licks at them, rubs them together, pushes them so that they touch and then licks the cleft in between. She knows my cunt is begging to be touched, but she refuses. Instead, she snakes her tongue down there, licks the insides of my thighs, and stops just inches away from my clit. It is my reward for teasing her, and she won't even allow me to brush my pussy with my hand for relief. Instead, she goes back to sucking my nipples and pushing her tongue into my mouth.

My skin is alive and on fire with each touch of her brilliant fingers and tongue. Leslie is an expert at love-making, and it is a joy just to lie back and submit to her will. She paints fanciful designs on my belly with her tongue, coming closer to my hot mound with each sweep.

When she finally touches my clit, I cry out with pleasure. She has somehow managed to focus my whole body on this point, and she shows me no mercy as she licks and sucks me. Her tongue is hot and wet between my legs, licking my clit, her hot breath playing on my aching skin. She pushes her finger into my hole as she licks me and begins moving it in and out, fucking me with her hand. It drives me wild and I cry for her to lick me harder. Her hand moves faster, her fingers deep inside me, her whole hand wet with my juice, her tongue lapping at me. My orgasm catches me by surprise. The wave of feeling moves right out to my toes and fingertips. When it is finished, I cannot bear to have her touch me. It is as if my skin is gone, and the nerves are on the edge of my flesh. Like her, I quiver and shake, and finally calm down in the loving circle of her arms.

The problem with making love in the early afternoon, of course, is that not much else gets done the rest of the day. With the cool sea breezes coming in through the window and both of us basking in our orgasms, we fall asleep in each other's arms. When I finally wake up, the shadows from the plants in the window are stretched long across the floor.

I try to get up without waking her, but it is no use; her enormous blue eyes open as soon as I sit up. I hold her tightly and kiss her beautiful lips. Our bodies are cooler now and it feels good to press against her, our breasts held tightly together, our pubic hair mingling. She brushes a lock of dark hair out of my eyes and kisses me again.

We dress and walk downstairs; I have offered to treat for dinner. We walk along the house-lined street, hand in hand, and every now and again I stop to admire the front yards. In Provincetown, gardening seems to be a way of life, and almost every house is decorated with beautifully kept, colorful flower gardens. Their vibrant shades contrast sharply with my Florida home, where houses are more commonly landscaped with palms and shrubs. The colors remind me of Leslie, so vibrant and alive. She often paints the rich gardens and it seems as if she puts her soul into the colors too; one of her gardens hangs in my trailer where it brightens my isolated winter months.

We stop for dinner in one of the many open-air sidewalk restaurants. Over an aperitif she tells me about an idea she has for a new painting, and I feel a quick pang when I realize it will probably be finished and sold before I return in the spring. Many of her paintings are sold out of the gallery below my apartment, and when she is busy working I sometimes wander downstairs and study them. Like her seashell trinkets, I can see her in them: sensuous, earthy, firmly attached to this piece of land that juts sharply out into the bay. Her works are so unlike my writing, with its wanderlust, its ever-changing horizons.

Feeling like a tourist, I order a clambake dinner. I am still high from our afternoon sex, yet I want her again so badly my pussy throbs and I rub against the hard plastic chair. Still, I am tempered by the knowledge that our summer is coming to a close, and I know how hard it will be to say good-bye to her. I take out some of my frustration by cracking the steamed clamshells sharply in half, and breaking the lobster shell loudly with the steel crackers.

Leslie enjoys a much quieter dinner of crab cakes. Each time she lifts the fork to her lips, her tongue darts out first to meet it. I can feel myself getting wet and swollen at the sight, and I imagine that tongue in my mouth, in my pussy, against my hard, aching nipples.

She sees the look in my eyes, and reaches under the table to squeeze my knee. The tablecloth is very long and with a mischievous grin, she lightly runs her fingernails up and down my thigh, putting her finger under the edge of my shorts to tickle the skin underneath.

Gradually she moves her hand up further. My lobster is quickly forgotten. Under the cover of the tablecloth, she twists her hand to push my legs apart, then moves back and forth near my crotch in her lovely, teasing manner. I can hardly believe I'm sitting in a crowded restaurant with Leslie's hand near my cunt, and I pick up my wine glass and sip at it in a foolish attempt to look natural.

The waiter comes by and asks if everything is fine. Still with her impish grin, Leslie answers yes and at the same time, rubs her thumb over my swollen clit. The waiter glances up at my sharp intake of breath, but I smile and nod at him. I am relieved when he moves away to another table. Leslie winks at me, like a schoolgirl playing a prank, and takes a forkful of her dinner. Meanwhile, her other hand is busy teasing and stroking my throbbing pussy.

She starts rubbing my clit right through my shorts, which are very thin, and I can feel each flicker of her finger over me. I am having a hard time holding still. I want to writhe on her hand, squirm in the seat, push her hand against myself and hold it tight to me. Leslie knows this, and she is having a grand time watching me trying vainly to control my movements. I warn her that she will be teased without mercy for this. She only laughs and increases the motion on my hot button.

I can feel the heat from my belly right down to my thighs. Leslie plays me like an instrument, knowing just when to rub hard and when to pull back and gently caress. Any attempt at sipping my wine is forgotten. I feel as if the whole restaurant must know what's going on, but I'm beyond caring. All that matters is my lover's hand touching me. I tighten up, so close, so close, and then the hot, sweet wave rises up out of my pussy and moves up my spine in a rapid, blissful sweep. I bite my tongue to keep from crying out as I come. Leslie's hand rubs every last wave out of my cunt, and I can feel that my shorts are soaked with my hot juice.

I struggle to pull myself together. Playing the saint, but with a canary-swallowing grin, Leslie is now eating her carrots, the picture of poise and manners. Orgasms always relax me and I seem to need all of my strength just to lift my hands and finish eating my dinner. Luckily for me the lobster is done, for the effort would have been far too much to handle. The potato is work enough at this stage.

When coffee comes, Leslie orders a slice of cheesecake, and is right back at it again, nibbling at it and running her tongue over the fork when she slides it out of her mouth. She is an angel to me; no woman I have ever met loves sex as much as she does, or makes me want her more. When we are together, I feel as if our only purpose on earth is to love and satisfy each other.

It is dusk by the time we finally finish. The street-lights are on and the shop windows are lit up, all of them open until very late to catch the tourist trade. The streets are alive with people walking along the sidewalks and up the middle of the narrow, one-way street. We decide it is too nice a night to let slip away, and we go for a stroll ourselves.

Provincetown was built for walking. Cars defer to pedestrians here, and drivers will usually follow a group of walkers slowly down the road rather than honk and demand that they move. Bicycles are of course another matter, and Leslie and I check carefully for any before we cross over the street. The sidewalks are wide and couples walk arm in arm, men with men, women with women, women with men. There is an easy summer feel to the place, mixed with an almost overwhelming sexual satisfaction. On a warm night like this, it feels as if everyone in town is going to be happily fucked before dawn, no matter what their preference.

We stop off in the bookstore, where both of us buy a couple of volumes. We chat for a while with the shopkeeper, who knows us well—both of us seem to spend half our income on books. When we leave, we run into another pair of friends who invite us to a nearby bar for a drink.

The bar is cool and dark, with jazz playing quietly

on the sound system. I am torn in my desire; I enjoy sitting and talking with our friends, but I am dying to get home and pay Leslie back for making me come in the restaurant. As we are sitting down, I brush against her and take advantage of the opportunity to tweak her nipple. She gives me a sultry smile across the table and I know she is just as eager to be paid back.

We order a carafe of wine. Our friends are a bit older than we are, two women who have lived together in Provincetown for years. Leslie sees them frequently over the winter, and often has dinner with them. As for me, they are two of the people I am sorry to leave when I make my trip back south.

As we talk, I can't keep my eyes off Leslie. A year younger than me, her blonde hair is bleached almost white from the hours of scouring the beaches for shells. She has the lovely outdoorsy look of people who live with hot summers, icy winters and the relentless tides. Her breasts are small and firm; I can still feel her nipple hot under my fingers. Her legs are long, her feet thrust into well-worn sandals. She still wears her thin shorts, and my eyes trace up the lines of her bare thighs to where they meet at her honey-rich, blonde pussy. I can picture how beautiful it looks, and I long to be there, rubbing my fingers, licking with my tongue....

I feel a hand on my arm, and realize that I have been spoken to but am off in my sexual dream world. All three of them laugh. I explain that I'm tired because of long nights pummeling my book into shape, but Leslie smiles knowingly at me. It's not much of a secret, what I'm actually thinking about.

It seems to take forever for the wine to be finished. I engage in conversation, but all the time, my mind is riveted on making love to my Leslie. Two women at a nearby table lean over it so close that their faces touch and they kiss gently; below the table they have their hands on each other's legs. I want desperately to touch Leslie like that. I can taste her juices in my mouthful of wine. In the midst of conversation she reaches over to take my hand, to make a point. Her warm skin is electric on mine.

Finally the wine is finished, and we beg off, explaining that I need some sleep. We kiss them good-bye and head back down the busy street to my apartment. On the way I lean over for a quick kiss, which turns passionate very quickly. Leslie is just as much in need as I am. We duck into a narrow alleyway between two stores. Her tongue is in my mouth immediately, probing and pressing against mine as hard as she can. She takes my hand and guides it between her legs. I can feel her wetness through her shorts, and her flesh seems on fire. She moans and rubs against my hand, her fingers on my breasts through my shirt. We grope like two sex-starved teenagers, kissing, feeling, grabbing each other with only one thing in mind. Reluctantly, I break away and take her hand, pulling her quickly along the crowded sidewalks. I can't get home fast enough, and Leslie keeps up with me.

There is a pleasant surprise waiting. The art gallery has rearranged its window, and one of Leslie's paintings hangs in front. It is a vibrant nude woman, her full breasts tipped with pink erect nipples, her hand gently exploring the dark triangle between her legs. The face is very abstract, but Leslie told me that she painted it while thinking of me. Seeing it out in the open, studied carefully by the people in the street who stop to look at it, makes me even hotter. I want to proudly tell them that it is my Leslie's work, that it is our wonderful sex set down in oils for everyone to admire.

I unlock the door and we go up the stairs, stopping halfway up for another long, passionate kiss. Usually I stop at my desk each time I enter the apartment, if only for a few moments, to proofread a page or add a couple of lines to the sheet that's always in the typewriter. This time, I ignore all of it.

We undress each other. Leslie comes up behind me and hugs me tightly. Her hands reach for me. Her right hand cups my breast. Her left hand moves down and her finger fits perfectly into the groove of my pussy lips. She plants delicate kisses on my neck while she fingers me. I reach behind and grab her ass cheeks, pulling her sweet mound close to my body. I can feel her heat from here.

She leads me to the bed. I make her lie face down on the comforter and kneel beside her. She loves to have her back rubbed as a prelude to sex. I start at her neck, rubbing gently, feeling her sweet skin move beneath my fingers. Gradually I work my way down her spine, kneading the soft flesh around her shoulders. Every now and again I bend down and trace the curve of her spine with my tongue, burying deep in the indentation just above her ass. She sighs and begs me to touch her pussy, but I tease her instead by just brushing the blonde hairs around it.

When I reach her ass, I spend a long time kneading her firm, creamy cheeks. Then I lean down and gently tongue the cleavage between them. She moans and lifts her hips to meet me. I brush her soft pussy hair again, this time with my tongue. As a final tease, I lick just once over her hot, wet cunt. She groans and rolls over, begging me to make her come.

It's too soon for that. Her beautiful tits are now facing me, and I waste no time in getting to them. I lick and suck at them, then push my own against them. Rubbing my nipples against hers gets both of us even hotter, and my pussy is throbbing with a will of its own.

She moans and kneads my breasts, and we deep-kiss for a long time, holding each other's nipples and rolling them between our fingers. Her touch sends hot shivers through me. I reach down and cup her steamy pussy in my hand.

Leslie pushes against my hand, trying to brush her clit against me. I touch the hot button quickly, brushing it with the tips of my fingers. She moans. She knows how to get to me, and plays with my nipples until I can't control myself any longer. I reach down and sink my tongue into her gorgeous cunt.

Immediately she bucks her hips up to push her clit against my tongue. Her pussy is as sweet as always. I take my time, using the very tip of my tongue to run under her soft folds all the way around to her lovely clit and hole.

She pulls at me, and I stop long enough to move over and straddle her lips with my own hot cunt. We both love "sixty-nine," and waste no time in feasting on each other. I like it because I am so busy concentrating on eating her, it takes a while for me to come and I can enjoy the achingly beautiful buildup even longer.

I am sure the gallery patrons below can hear us, we are moaning and lapping so loudly. For a while Leslie mirrors all of my actions. When I slow down and circle her pussy, she does the same to mine. Flicking my tongue hard across her clit brings the same hot flashes across my own. It is almost as if I am eating myself.

There is a new sensation now; Leslie's fingers are deep in my cunt, her tongue still on my clit. I love the full feeling, the way her thumb moves to brush against the folds of skin. I do the same to her. Her tight tunnel is soaked and feverishly hot. I fuck her with my fingers while I concentrate my tongue on her swollen clit.

Both of us madly enjoy our lickfest a little while longer. Then Leslie asks me to move down on the bed, which I do. Her hair dishevelled and her pussy wetly glistening, she positions herself opposite me, her legs crossed scissor-style over mine. Our two pussies touch and she begins to rub against me.

I push hard to match her frantic motions. I pull myself up on my pillow so I can see, and it's gorgeous. My own dark triangle grinds against her blonde one, clits nestled together, juices flowing. I love the scratchy feeling of her hair against me. She pushes hard and I gasp.

We start a regular rhythm. Hips bucking, soft pussies grinding into each other, we moan and gasp at the waves of pleasure that course through our bodies. Her leg is stretched along my body and I take her foot, planting kisses on it. I push my tongue between her toes and she moans, grinding even harder. I match her movements.

We are moving so fast and hard I expect our cunts to burst into flame. Mine is already on fire, heating me, tongues of flame moving up my spine as her sweet bush crushes me. Both of us are sitting up now, taking in the beautiful sight of two cunts pressing together, dark and light hair, creamy asses, outstretched legs.

Leslie moves frantically and begins to cry out. She comes violently, her juices flooding my pussy. I have never felt so wet. She moans and shivers, enjoying every last wave, pushing against me. I get even hotter watching her come.

She waits for only a moment, then gracefully pulls away from me and kneels before my cunt, spreading my legs. Her practiced fingers begin to stroke my pussy. Her hand feels as good as her hot cunt did against my flesh.

She rubs faster and faster, her finger slipping over my soaked clit. Then she slips two fingers inside my hole, while her thumb expertly rubs the swollen button. She is a master, sliding in and out of my cunt, rubbing me, while her free hand reaches up to knead my breast.

I can't believe how intense my orgasm is. I seem to come from the very tips of my toes, and Leslie rides me out. Her thumb plays out all of it, until I am weak and gasping. Then she is in my arms, kissing my face, cupping my tender pussy with her hand.

I return her kiss. I can't believe how much I love her and how good she makes me feel. We lie together on the bed, our bodies covered in sweat and pussy juice. The smell of sex is heavy in the air.

Through the open window I can hear people talking as they walk by on the sidewalk. I wonder if anyone heard our loud lovemaking. I like to think that they did.

Gently, Leslie kisses me on the lips, then snuggles down within the curve of my arm, her head resting on my shoulder. One finger absently traces circles around my nipple. I turn my head and gently kiss her forehead.

There is no question of her staying the night; I am not about to let go of her right now. She pulls the light cover over us, since neither of us seems to have the strength to get up and close the window. We say a silent prayer to the inventor of the remote control, as I click on the small television that sits atop a book-shelf. We reject a talk show, a half-hour commercial for car wax and a police drama, and finally settle on my favorite movie, *Casablanca*, already halfway through. No matter, it's worth watching from any point. We both admit that we love Ingrid Bergman's clothes, sultry eyes and beautifully full, kissable lips, and not necessarily in that order.

Unfortunately, I miss my opportunity to see Bogie put her on the plane, for the next thing I know the early morning sunlight is streaming through the window and Leslie is clattering cups in my cramped kitchen. She kisses me good morning and deposits a cup of strong black coffee on the nightstand beside me.

Always an early riser, she is dressed with her cup of coffee half finished. She hugs me tightly and tells me she has to get home to finish a piece that the gallery is waiting for. My heart sinks when I hear the door close behind her, for the breeze coming through the open window has an end-of-season chilly touch to it.

I smooth the bed, pull on my jeans and take my coffee to the typewriter. Just after one o'clock, I am finished. Once again I am filled with the same conflicting emotions that I always feel when I start to pack a book for shipping to the publisher: elation that it's finally finished, but an emotional drain knowing that the work I've been doing for so long is over.

I call Leslie to tell her, but I get her answering machine. When she is working she turns it all the way down so that she can't hear the messages. I tell her there will be victory champagne later, then I wrap the book carefully for mailing and address it.

I walk into the downtown center with the precious parcel in my arms. The breeze is coming in over the ocean heavily, and it feels like rain, but I don't care. I mail the book inside the huge old post office building, then continue walking until I am out of town, up at the sand dunes that separate the waves from the road.

There is another couple walking along the beach, two women, arm in arm. I sit down on the soft sand and watch them. They stop to look at the sky and the waves, to pick up shells on the sand. They are an older couple, gray-haired but moving as gracefully as women half their age. They obviously know each other well, their motions complementing each other, their steps matching. I can see Leslie and myself together that way in twenty years, moving with the comfortable rhythm of people who understand each other perfectly.

Eventually the women gather their bicycles and walk back to the road, nodding a hello to me as they pass. I get up and walk down to the water's edge, catching a glimpse of a shell half-buried. I pick it up and rinse it in the ripple of water that moves up close to me. I know Leslie would like it, and I slip it into my pocket.

The air is very heavy and by the time I walk back to the road, there is a thin drizzle falling. In the way of seaside storms, it grows into heavy rain very quickly. There is no point in hurrying, and so I walk back toward the town with the rain beating down on me, my clothes soaked and sticking to my skin. When it runs down my face it feels like tears.

The rain is still falling steadily when I get back to my apartment. Leslie has obviously heard my message on her machine, for she is inside the gallery, looking through the open door and talking to the owner. She tells me to hurry up and get inside to some dry clothes.

It is difficult to peel the wet jeans off. When I do, I remember the shell, and I give it to Leslie, who is fascinated with it. She has already started to run a hot bath for me. I slip into the steaming tub, filled with richly scented bubbles; the hot water on my cold clammy skin is almost erotic.

When the bathwater starts to cool, Leslie comes back in. She holds a large fluffy bathtowel and I let her dry me off, almost purring with the luxury. Finally she wraps me in my sinfully thick terrycloth robe and we go into the kitchen.

She has brought steaks for dinner. Although the kitchen is tiny we work well together, like trained chefs. I boil rice while she washes vegetables and arranges the steaks on the broiling pan.

When dinner is on the table, I open the champagne bottle with a flourish and pour two glasses. We toast the book, then eat our dinners. Leslie tells me about her painting, which is almost finished, and I promise another bottle of champagne.

After dinner we clear the table and I run hot water into the sink. But before I can start washing dishes, I feel Leslie come up behind me and slip her arms around my waist. I turn, and meet her open-mouthed, sweet kiss.

The dishes are instantly forgotten as she unties my robe and opens it. Her hand slips down expertly to my breasts and fondles my nipples. I moan and kiss at her mouth, my hand slipping between her legs to feel her pussy through her jeans.

She breaks away and leads me into the bedroom. The familiar bed is inviting and we lie down together, kissing deeply and smoothing our hands over each other's creamy soft skin. I want to get inside her, in her mouth, in her pussy, under her skin, I love her and want her so much.

She is down and working my pussy over before I even realize it. The warmth from her wet tongue radiates through my thighs and up my spine. She licks me slowly, carefully, as if I am ice cream or a forbidden sweet treat. It is as hot and intense as the warm bathwater on my cold skin.

I can only groan and go limp with the pleasure. I let the delicious feeling of Leslie's tongue in my pussy take me over. She licks my thighs and the outer lips of my cunt, then zeros in on my clit with just the very tip of her tongue. Her touch is as light as her warm breath on me, and it tickles wonderfully, like she is stroking me with a feather.

She alternates for a while, rubbing my pussy with her fingers, then licking me slowly with her tongue. I love the motion of her hand, soft yet firm on my throbbing, wet clit, followed by the fluid movements of her swift tongue. I could lie back and take this for hours, it feels so good. She knows it, and she laps at me with long wet strokes from my hole right up to my clit. I shudder with each juicy sweep.

Leslie sits up for a moment and reaches for the glass of chilled champagne she has brought into the bedroom with her. She takes a mouthful and holds it for a moment, then swallows and returns to my aching pussy.

I gasp at the first touch of her icy tongue. Delicious little shivers course through me. I can hardly believe the sensation, her cold tongue and her hot breath mingling together on my cunt. Gradually her tongue warms up, and I cry for more. She takes another sip of the pale golden wine, and once again I am treated to her sweet cold tongue and warm breath, icy-hot between my legs.

My own mouth wants her now, to share this new feeling. Reluctantly she stops and stretches out in front of me. I take a sip from her glass, then move down to the blonde pussy that I want so very badly. Like me, she moans at the fiercely cold movement on her erect little button, and she asks for seconds when my tongue warms up again on her beautiful clit.

I sip more champagne, then bend down to her beautiful pussy. I can't get enough of her. I lick her pussy lips, nibble her clit gently. She moans and pushes against my tongue. I know from experience just what she likes best, and I give it to her, little butterfly kisses on her clit, my tongue stuck deep into her hole.

I want to make her come. I concentrate on her clit now, my tongue pressed against it. I can feel her excitement as she runs her fingers through my hair and pushes me deep into her sweet lips. Faster and faster I lick her, while she gasps and squirms on the bed. Finally she cries out with her release, her hips moving as I push my tongue into her.

Leslie begs me to kiss her, so that she can taste her juices on my tongue. I move up on the bed and hold her close, kissing her and sharing what I have done with her. It is like sharing a beautiful intimate secret.

My own pussy is still throbbing sharply. As we kiss, Leslie's hand strays to it, and I moan at the first touch of her fingers. She plays with me, still kissing me. Our breasts are pressed tightly together and I love her hard nipples so close to mine.

She asks me to kneel over her. I do, positioning my pussy over her lips. She reaches up and grabs my ass cheeks, pulling me down to her mouth. The touch of her tongue on my swollen clit is magical.

She knows me as well as I know her. She licks the spots that excite me the most and then, when I am built up and almost overcome with the sensation, she concentrates on a less sensitive area. As always she loves to tease and on this afternoon she is doing a magnificent job.

Finally she flicks her tongue hard on my clit, the movement that she knows will make me come. It doesn't take long to build up the pressure that I feel just before orgasm. Leslie licks faster and the waves roll through my legs and belly, hot tingling flashes that are just heavenly.

I move down on the bed beside her, and we snuggle in together under the light blanket. It seems as if we have spent all of our time in bed the last few days. Leslie quickly agrees that it doesn't seem to be a bad way to pass the time.

I hold her tightly in the half-lit room. We listen to the rain beating on the roof and the thunder that crashes overhead occasionally. I remember as a child lying in bed and feeling very secure and comfortable in my warm bed with the sounds of the rain outside. Holding Leslie close to me, I feel as content as I did then.

Gently, Leslie kisses me on the lips, then burrows down within the curve of my arm, her head resting on my shoulder. One finger absently traces circles around my nipple. I turn my head and kiss her forehead.

We hold each other very tightly, as if nothing could tear us apart. From below, we can hear the faint, muffled voices of people in the gallery, but we have no desire to join the outside world right now. For the moment, we are complete, lying together in the bed.

We talk for a long time, punctuating with tiny kisses. She tells me that she has always wanted to visit Disneyworld, and likes the idea of eating vine-ripened tomatoes in the middle of December.

I tell her I am thinking about setting my next book in a seaside town in the dead of winter. She listens carefully. We know we are both telling the truth.

"DEVON WHITFIELD"
(from *Private Lessons*)

Devon Whitfield is the headmistress of the Whitfield
Finishing Academy for Young Ladies, one of nineteenth-
century London's most prestigious boarding schools.
Unbeknownst to parents and to half of the students,
there are actually two curricula at the school: the everyday lessons learned by all, and the special "private
lessons" administered to select students by cruel and
dominant teachers.

The most recent group of students was doing
well, Devon decided, as she perused the
reports on her desk. She had asked all of the
teachers to submit at least one report on each of the
students, so that she, as headmistress, could send
letters to the parents of the girls reporting on their

progress, as she did periodically. She divided the reports into two piles.

One pile—the larger of the two—contained a page on each student which listed the students grades and comments on her education. Devon put these aside.

The second pile—not quite as large but still a very impressive size—contained reports that the parents would never see. Also penned by the teachers, they were much more interesting and would eventually go into the huge files that Devon kept for herself under lock and key.

She picked up the first one, noting the neat script of riding instructor Rebecca Briggs, herself a favorite with the headmistress of this most impressive finishing school.

"Regarding Amy Gates," the report began. "Miss Gates has been at the Academy for nine months now and has proven to be a very interesting student."

Devon smiled. Rebecca was as difficult to please as Devon was; her standards were almost impossibly high. Any student described by Rebecca as "interesting" was bound to be delightful.

She is a young blond student, well fleshed; and this led me to believe that her asscheeks would be very creamy and nice to spank. The first time I had reason to bring her in for discipline, and to haul up her skirts and pull down her drawers, I immediately saw that I was correct. Her sweet buttocks are like the finest ivory, and even sweeter in that they go a brilliant shade of red once the hairbrush is applied. She is somewhat tolerant of pain, which is very good also, for a spanking may be carried on and on before she starts to cry and scream. Her little cunny is very blond also, and gets wet when she is spanked. I believe that if I were to allow it, I could bring her to a peak simply by smacking her sweet ass long enough.

Of course, spanking is not the only thing I have discovered with this young wench. Her breasts are very firm and pert, and her nipples respond well to being squeezed hard; in fact, they seem to erect themselves at my lightest touch. One evening I placed clips upon them and left them there for almost three-quarters of an hour; but even though Miss Gates was obviously in distress, she did not cry for them to be removed.

I have inflicted almost every punishment at my disposal upon her. She responds well to the riding crop, to the buggy whip, and to that delicious whip that you keep in the discipline chamber. As for paddles, she is divine. Although, the wooden and rubber ones worked well, the metal-studded one was the finest, as that beautiful white skin came up in dots of red. Eventually, after repeated paddling, her sweet fanny was covered with a lovely red rash from the marks of the studs overlapping with each blow.

While I do not wish to influence your judgment in any way, I would heartily suggest that this student not be moved forth at the end of the semester, but kept from her home and retained here at the Academy. If you require a cause, I will state that while her hands are good, her seat in the saddle is not yet perfect. I implore you, for your own pleasure, not to send this student forth until you have personally enjoyed her young breasts and fleshy buttocks. I assure you that you will not be disappointed.

> *Your obedient servant, Rebecca Briggs.*

Devon smiled. She enjoyed Rebecca's reports most

of all. Among all the teachers, Rebecca put the most thought and care into her prose and insisted on relating every intoxicating detail. Devon made a note to herself to find Amy Gates guilty of some infraction and have the pleasure of calling her into the office and experiencing for herself the satisfaction that the riding teacher had so obviously enjoyed herself on more than one occasion.

She was just about to pick up another report when there was a gentle knock at the door. Annoyed, she called out, "Who is it?"

The heavy oak door opened slowly, just a little, and a young female face appeared behind it. Devon recognized her immediately: Lilian Smith, a student whom Devon had had the pleasure of disciplining herself on a number of occasions.

"What do you want?" Devon demanded.

Lilian stepped into the room, dropping her eyes to the floor and performing the required curtsy before speaking. "Please, Mistress Whitfield," she said. "Mistress Briggs requests the pleasure of your company."

"Where?"

"In the chamber, Mistress," the young woman replied.

Devon's eyebrows rose. "In her private chamber?"

"No, Mistress," Lilian replied, and she caught her breath. "In the discipline chamber."

So the morning would be an interesting one, Devon decided. She looked at the young messenger, whose cheeks had flushed scarlet at the mention of the special room on the very top floor. She had spent time in there herself, at the hands of her teachers and also Mistress Whitfield's. Half of her envied whichever student was up there now; half of her pitied the captive, who assured had done something very wrong to warrant such a measure. She could almost see the racks and feel her wrists pulled tightly together and shackled in place. How she wished she were there!

"Dismissed," Devon said. The young woman thanked her Mistress, then slipped out the door.

Devon put her papers away and stepped into the hallway. She still had time before her interview, and the treat waiting upstairs would fill it quite nicely.

The discipline chamber was only one of several rooms that comprised the top floor of the east wing. Access to all of them was through a single door which was always kept locked and could be opened only by the teachers and by Devon herself. Not all of the Academy's students received these special private lessons, and the locked door was intended to keep them out. It was also a valuable tool for punishing the students who did receive lessons; many reported that the sound of the door locking behind them and the walk to the discipline chamber down the long hall could be as terrible a treatment as the actual punishment itself. The teachers' living quarters were directly below the private wing, and that section was also protected by a lock and key. However, there were sufficient secret passageways from the top floor to the one below, to best accommodate the teachers and their pleasure.

Devon opened the door with her key, then firmly closed and locked it behind her. The long hallway, with its huge window at one end, was all gleaming mahogany, smelling faintly of the lemon oil rubbed in by submissive students who begged to do the job on their hands and knees—mostly naked, as ordered by their dominatrices. The magnificent oil paintings that graced the other halls of the Academy were noticeably missing here. Instead, the walls were sparsely but effectively decorated with the tools the teachers loved to use behind closed doors. Here was a riding crop, a rug beater; farther down the hallway hung a pair of leather wrist-cuffs shackled together, and a bridle specially made to fit a young woman's face. Beside the door to the discipline chamber was Devon's favorite; a beautifully executed drawing of a young woman across her Mistress's knee, with her bare buttocks exposed and her tormentor's hand raised to deliver a stinging slap.

But today this was just an appetizer for the feast that waited inside. Devon opened the door to this most delightful chamber and stepped inside.

The chamber itself was a huge room, with windows on two sides that could be covered with heavy velvet drapes. Today they were open, and the sunlight revealed the room's secrets. In the center were several wooden horses, a table with iron hooks screwed into it, and a horrible wooden rack which could accommodate two slaves, one on either side of it. Along the walls were more racks, huge iron rings, shelves filled with all manner of toys and devices, and a row of comfortable stuffed chairs for an audience. Unknown to any of the students who had been enslaved in here, there were also holes in the west wall, hidden amid the ornate carvings of the wainscoting, and a small hidden chamber in behind them where teachers and guests could watch the proceedings in the room without their presence being known.

The tall ceiling was crossed with huge oak beams, into which were screwed several large iron rings. From two of these hung young ladies, their wrists shackled together and then tethered to the rings. They were pulled up just far enough that they were barely able to keep their toes on the highly polished floor. Both of them wore their long skirts and petticoats, with no shoes or stockings, but they were naked from the waist up, their breasts pulled up and their nipples sweet and rosy.

"Mistress Whitfield! How good of you to come!" Rebecca Briggs was seated in one of the chairs, admiring the two nubile creatures that dangled so enticingly from their cruel bonds. She stood up and walked over to the door where Devon waited. She was a beautiful woman who moved with an easy grace and a long-legged stride. For this occasion she was wearing hunting attire, and her tight-fitting jodhpurs and tailored shirt complemented the stern leather boots she wore. Like Devon, she wore men's riding clothes whenever she could, for she also knew the secret pleasures of mounting astride.

"How good of you to ask me," Devon said. She admired Rebecca, admired her cold, firm eyes and the set of her jaw that intimidated all of the students below her. Rebecca's beautiful body and dominant ways made her a favorite with Devon among all the teachers, both as a disciplinarian and also, in the privacy of their chambers, as a lover.

"You have set them up very nicely," Devon continued. She walked over to them. Both of the girls were trembling now; for, as harsh as Rebecca was, she was no match for Devon and her punishments, and the captives knew this.

Devon reached forward and touched the nipple of one of the girls. The young woman drew in her breath, and her face went red. Devon moved her hand so that she cupped the firm young globe and massaged it. The girl's breathing increased. It sounded improbably loud in the empty room.

It feels so good, doesn't it?" Devon asked.

The girl nodded her head slightly and whispered, "Yes, Mistress," so softly that it was almost inaudible.

Devon continued to play with the girl's breast, with both hands now, one hand tweaking the nipple and the other massaging the flesh. She could feel the flesh hot in her palm and hear the maiden's breathing. The other captive watched, longing for her Mistress's hands to be on her body.

Straining on her toes, the young girl was panting in the way that indicated she was close to her peak. Devon looked at her and smiled coldly. Then she gave the tit a final squeeze and stepped away. Crestfallen, frustrated, the young woman panted and for a moment considered begging for more, but suddenly remembered her place and held her tongue.

"What were their transgressions?" Devon asked.

"Improper care of their charges," Rebecca replied. "The one on the left was in a hurry when she came back from her ride, so she hurried her horse's brushing and missed several strokes. As for the one on the right, I found some dirt on her saddle when it was supposed to have been cleaned."

"Serious charges," Devon said.

"Serious indeed," Rebecca agreed. "And deserving of punishment. That is why I thought you would like to be here, to witness their humiliation."

Rebecca went to the shelves that held the implements. Two pairs of eyes, wide with fear, followed her movements as she selected a heavy whip and brought it back with her.

The young woman who had been frustrated by Devon's touch was first. The whip snapped across her back, and she clenched her teeth together so that only a grunt escaped. Devon beamed. The cruel lash left a delicious red welt across the girl's pale back.

A similar stripe was raised along the spine of the other girl. Then Rebecca began a regular routine; one lash on the first back, one lash on the second. Soon both backs were striped with lashes, and the girls were screaming for mercy, tears streaming down their cheeks. Of course it was pointless. No one could hear them here, save the two Mistresses who savored every desperate cry for help.

Finally Rebecca decided that the punishment was complete, and she took the whip back to the shelves. The girls still hung by their wrists, sobbing, battered and tear-stained. Without a word, Rebecca loosed their bonds, and they dropped to the floor, their legs too numb to hold them up. Devon thought they looked magnificent; their skirts disarrayed, their backs worked over, their bare nipples hard and pink.

"Now get out of here," Rebecca hissed. "Go to your classes, but once tea is over, you are to report back to me here."

"Yes, Mistress," the two replied. Stiffly, their backs burning with the red welts, they gathered up their blouses and left. Of course they would be blocked in their progress by the locked door at the end of the hall and forced to wait however long it would take for either Devon or Rebecca to open it for them. They only hoped that which ever Mistress it was, she would not be carrying a riding crop when she came out to open it. Their poor backs were sore enough, without their skirts being lifted and a harsh leather whip applied to their backsides!

"Another session with them after tea?" Devon asked.

"This whipping was for punishment, to correct their errors," Rebecca explained. "Later on there will be spanking, both to reinforce their lessons and to amuse me."

"A good idea," Devon agreed. "But remember that tomorrow is the day for our trip into town."

Rebecca smiled; her eyes were bright with anticipation. "Of course I have not forgotten," she assured the headmistress. "I have been looking forward to it all this month."

Devon reached forward and kissed her passionately, then turned to leave. "I, too, will enjoy tomorrow," she said. "But when you are finished with their spanking, Rebecca, you might come visit me in my own chamber. There's nothing like a little fun of our own to get us in the mood for a day's trip into town."

"RIKKI"
(from *Romantic Encounters*)

Julie Gray is the editor of a romance novel publishing house and has just signed the company's top-selling writer. She is determined to seduce this exciting, virginal writer; but in the meantime, on a cross-country tour to promote the novel, she decides that there's no use being celibate while she's waiting.

J ulie liked The Bengal because it attracted a wide range of women, and it was easy to have just about any kind of fantasy fulfilled if you took the time to work at it. She wasn't sure what kind of a mood she was in, but she was definitely mellow. The flight, the longing for her author, the fine dinner and now the good scotch had definitely smoothed her out, and the more she thought about it, the more she thought she would like to be taken. She was just too cool to be aggressive.

"I like the looks of that one over there." Madison gestured to a young woman sitting by herself at a small table.

"Go for it," Julie urged.

"I think I will," Madison said. "You mind? You okay by yourself?"

"Never been better," Julie said. "Just remember your buddy who hasn't got her virgin quite off the shelf yet."

"Bullshit!" Madison reached over and gave Julie a quick kiss. "A smoothie like you? I'm surprised she made it over on the flight with her pants still on."

She patted Julie's knee, then took her drink and walked across the floor. Julie watched as her delightful blonde friend introduced herself to the young woman, and then waited to be invited to sit down. She was, and Julie looked on admiringly as Madison slipped into the chair smoothly and started to talk. Was Madison a great publicist because she could talk so easily to people, or was her ability a result of her job? Whichever way it worked, Julie had never met anyone who could make a move on another woman the way Madison could. There was no doubt she wouldn't be sleeping alone this night.

No sooner had Madison left her stool than another woman got up from one of the back booths and walked over. "Taken?" She pointed to the empty stool, and when Julie shook her head, the woman put her bottle of beer on the bar and sat down.

Julie looked her up and down. She was a young woman, tall, lithe, whip-thin. Her hair was bleached pure white and razor-cut into a brush so short that from a distance she looked bald. Her features were so finely drawn that the severe look suited her. She wore no makeup and her skin was very pale. Both of her ears were pierced with several gold rings.

Her clothes were rough and punky. A tight tank showed off small, hard breasts with huge nipples, and the outline of a small ring through one of them. She wore black shorts that ended just below her ass, and her pale legs were bare. Her feet were clad in heavy socks and laced leather boots. Julie felt overdressed beside her. This rough dyke was intriguing, turning her on.

"Your girlfriend turned on you?" the woman asked. Her voice was hard, her words clipped.

"She's my co-worker," Julie explained. "We're in town for the night and we're finding our own."

"My name's Rikki," the pale woman said, taking a drink of her beer.

"Julie Gray," Julie said.

"Rikki's all you need from me," she replied. Instead of feeling rebuffed, Julie surprisingly found herself drawn toward Rikki. Already mellow, she didn't mind being drawn under this hard woman's spell at all.

"So you're out to find your own, you said?"

"Well, I'm not here for the show," Julie said, looking toward the band on-stage, who were doing a very poor version of an obscure Elvis song.

Rikki took another drink of her beer. "I'm a snatchlicker," she said. "Those are my terms."

"Fine with me," Julie said. "Do you have a place?" Her own suite was huge and undoubtedly more comfortable, but she didn't want to take Rikki there. For one thing, Rikki's unorthodox appearance would raise eyebrows from the staff, and Julie wasn't in the mood for that. More than that, though, she was getting right into the idea of giving in to Rikki's control. Almost always on top, always the leader, occasionally she liked to hand everything over and be swept away in whatever direction her lover cared to take her. She didn't want to take Rikki to the hotel with her; she wanted to be taken.

Rikki sighed. "Yeah, I've got a place," she said. Julie got the impression that her good clothes hinted at an expensive room that Rikki might have wanted to share, but it was too late. She was Rikki's now. "Drink up," the pale woman said, as she swallowed the last of her beer and got up from the stool.

Julie could see that Madison was also heading toward the door, the young girl walking in front of her. Madison saw her friend walking with the tall, tough blonde woman, but said nothing. There would be plenty of time in the morning to compare notes. For now, Julie wanted only one thing: Rikki's long, thin tongue on her cunt. All else would be in good time. She walked through the door that Rikki held open for her, and watched as the pale woman reached up one long, thin arm to signal for a cab. Julie looked about the darkened street with longing. For just a moment, she was a virgin herself once more.

The ride through the dark city streets was uneventful, save for the cabbie's own peculiar understanding of traffic lights and his puzzled expression every time he glanced at the two women in his rearview mirror.

Julie couldn't blame him. They certainly were an unusual couple: Julie well-dressed, her mane of blonde hair combed carefully, sitting upright; while slumped against the far door, Rikki was the picture of punk indifference. She had put on a worn black leather biker's cap that dipped insolently over one eye, and her shirt was pulled down so that the nipple with its piercing ring had all but slipped out over the top of it. Her long legs, with their heavy-soled, high-laced leather boots, were spread wide within the confines of the cab's interior, which was too short to accommodate her lankiness. Julie was completely taken with her.

They stopped in front of a small six-story apartment building that was just about to cross the line into well-aged squalor. Rikki paid the driver and they got out of the cab. The street was deserted, but the ever-present New York white noise was evident all around them, of voices from unseen apartments, music, a dog barking, a faraway siren. Julie felt like an actress in a movie as she followed Rikki up the short flight of cement stairs into the building.

They walked up to the second floor. The hallways were poorly lit, and Julie's shoes clicked on the floor. Rikki's keys hung off a heavy chain attached to her belt. She opened two locks on the door, then reached inside to turn on the light switch.

It was a singles apartment, small, cramped, well-worn, but surprisingly clean. The furnishings consisted of an old overstuffed sofa, a wing chair obviously rescued from a thrift shop, a battered dresser and a single bed, its sheets rumpled invitingly. There was a large, expensive stereo system, but no television. As Julie had expected, decorations consisted of large posters for little-known bands, and British and Confederate flags served as curtains.

One thing she did find surprising was a very large

bookcase, completely filled with finely bound books that had obviously been well read. She had to smile, though, when she noticed that three volumes on the lower shelf were from Sapphic Press; but she decided to keep her identity a secret.

The room was already quite warm, and the radiator rattled. Again, Julie was surprised; it was cool outside, but Rikki hadn't seemed the least bit chilled in her shorts. Julie took off her light coat but still felt hot. At first she was uncomfortable, but when Rikki walked over and opened one window a few inches, the cool air gave her a heady rush. The light-headed, feverish feeling only added to the intensity of being in this forbidding, claustrophobic room with this dangerous woman.

Rikki walked to the middle of the room, making sure that Julie's eyes were on her. She took off the biker's cap and tossed it on the bed. Her hair and skin seemed even whiter in the harsh overhead light. She was very posed, very careful. Julie knew that despite the seeming indifference, she was watching a carefully choreographed performance designed specifically for a wanting audience.

Julie was indeed wanting. She could feel that her satin panties were saturated with juice, and they were hot and heavy between her legs. When she held her thighs close together, the skin slipped effortlessly against itself, lubricated with pussynectar. Julie's clit was throbbing, and the heat of her lust went right through her belly and radiated through her body. So Rikki was a snatchlicker? Julie couldn't imagine wanting anything more. She wanted her snatch licked, sucked, probed. She wanted desperately to be eaten out. It was all she could do to keep from putting her hands between her legs and touching the hot flesh there.

Rikki knew this with a wisdom well beyond her years. She writhed her graceful body for Julie's benefit, showing off her litheness and her tough, almost masculine femininity. Her breasts were small and hard, her arms muscled, her legs firm. Her stomach was washboard-flat under the tight tank top. Her hands, though long and fine, bore evidence of hard work.

Then she pulled her shirt out of the waistband of the shorts, and held the bottom of it. Suddenly out of character, she smiled at Julie and winked. In one smooth, rapid movement she pulled the shirt over her head and stood before Julie, her chest naked. Julie's eyes went wide and involuntarily she let out a gasp. The sheer beauty overwhelmed her.

Under her shirt, Rikki was almost completely tattooed. The designs were closely done, richly colored, finely drawn with the tiniest of needles. All across her body, front and back, were images of women. It was unbelievable.

Julie could only stare as Rikki revolved slowly in front of her. There were kohl-eyed Egyptian queens and platinum-haired movie vamps. Naked women, their bodies in perfect proportion, kissed each other. Her back was dominated by a bathing beauty in the style of Vargas. On her torso was a fairy princess straight from the pages of a Victorian storybook. Her gossamer wings stretched up to encompass each of Rikki's nipples, one pierced by a gold ring with a pearl set into it. All of it was done so that even a sleeveless shirt revealed none of the artistry below. It was Rikki's secret, to bestow only on those she permitted to see it. The designs disappeared below the waistband of her shorts, and Julie longed to see the rest of them, but Rikki did not offer to display anything more.

"Exquisite!" Julie whispered.

"Of course," Rikki said, and although she sounded indifferent, Julie could detect just a hint of pride. There was just cause, of course, for the tattoos were amazing and had been done by the hand of a true master in the art. Julie, who had always been fascinated by this most intimate and permanent expression, felt her pussy sopping at the sight of them. Between the weightless design of the wing surrounding the nipple and the ring that went through it, she was almost crazy with wanting to suck on it; but she knew that this would not be possible. She had agreed to Rikki's conditions, so she had to content herself with admiring the designs. They were so close and so carefully done that it looked as if Rikki was wearing a second shirt, and Julie was amazed that no matter how much she looked, she was continually finding new pictures she hadn't noticed before.

Now Rikki came over to her and put her hands on either side of Julie's face. Her skin was extremely warm and Julie raised her hands to continue the embrace. Without a change of expression, Rikki moved back quickly, held Julie's wrists, and put them gently back at her sides. Not a word was spoken, but when Rikki resumed her touch on Julie's face, Julie forced herself to keep her hands at her sides. It was an unspoken agreement which Julie would keep. She had to. She wanted her pussy licked so badly, she could almost scream her desire, and she would do nothing right now to jeopardize the touch of a tongue on her clit.

Rikki opened the buttons of Julie's shirt slowly. For

this evening, Julie had worn no bra, and her breasts were immediately free of the clingy fabric. Rikki sucked one slowly into her mouth; Julie groaned as she felt Rikki's tongue on her sensitive nipple. Rikki was slow but thorough. With Julie's tit inside her mouth, she tongued a circle all around the crisp areola and teased the very end of the nipple. Julie felt her knees go weak as her cunt throbbed, but she stood straight, and reveled in the attention she was receiving from this delicious dyke.

Now Rikki moved to the other breast and gave it the same treatment. When she took her mouth away, she blew on it gently. Julie shivered as the saliva on her nipple went cold, then groaned as Rikki took it back into her hot mouth. Rikki's expression never changed, but it was obvious that she was thoroughly enjoying this as well. Julie longed to see her pussy, but Rikki kept on her shorts and the heavy leather boots; and this was a turn-on in its own way. Both of the women were naked from the waist up, Rikki still partially clad in the glory of her tattoos, but Julie knew that the shorts would remain while she would be stripped naked. It was thrilling to be in such a position. Always the victor, she was now the prize, to be taken at will, and Julie was loving this role reversal as much as she was Rikki's mouth on her sensitive tits, the mouth that was now making her pussy so hot she could barely stand it.

Rikki rose slowly and slipped Julie's shirt from her shoulders. She took a maddeningly long time to fold it carefully, so that it would not crease, and lay it across the back of the wing chair. Then she returned, standing behind Julie, and ran her fingers up and down the length of Julie's spine. She played with

Julie's thick hair and reached in front to tease Julie's nipples. Julie could feel the small, hard tits pressing against her back and it warmed her right through. The spot where Rikki's skin touched her felt as hot as flame.

Now Rikki was reaching in front, her fingers searching for the waistband of Julie's pants. She opened them slowly, expertly, and slid the pants over Julie's hips. At a touch on each of her ankles, Julie lifted each foot. Rikki slipped off each shoe and then the pant leg. The pants were folded with the same meticulous care as the shirt, and laid over the wing chair; the shoes were placed together below it, touching, arranged as a pair. Julie was now standing in only her panties, and she could feel how wet they were.

This was not missed on Rikki. "You've got a soaked little slit," she said, as she ran her fingers against the fabric. Julie sighed at the feathery touch on her pussy. "How long have you been wet?"

"Since the bar," Julie admitted.

"I'm not surprised. I knew you wanted me right from the start."

Ever so slowly, Rikki pulled the panties down. "A true blonde," she observed. Julie said nothing. "I'm not," Rikki continued, "but I'm not going to show you what it really is. Your pussy is the only one that's important now."

She pulled the panties down, but this time she did not place them with Julie's clothes; instead, they stayed around her ankles. Rikki, now kneeling on the floor, bent down and buried her face in them, breathing deeply. When she had had her fill, she worked her way slowly up Julie's legs, using her fingers and her tongue to trace designs right up her thighs.

Her first touch on Julie's clit was magical. Julie shivered and Rikki smiled as the tormented clit was finally given a reprieve. Julie was honestly surprised at herself; as horny as she'd been, she hadn't really known the true depth of her want. It was as if every nerve in her body was connected directly to that nub of flesh between her legs, and Rikki's tongue on it touched every muscle of her being.

Julie looked down. It was so hot: Rikki, with her spiky, all-but-shaven head between Julie's thighs, on her knees, her thick-soled boots and heavy shorts covering her, with those magnificent tattoos writhing over her back and curving around her sides to spread up to her hard tits. She didn't make a sound, but stayed right on Julie's cunt, thrusting her tongue slowly so that the tip of it neatly parted the slit between Julie's pussylips. When she pulled back, she sucked Julie's cuntlips into her mouth and nibbled on them ever so gently until Julie moaned.

Rikki could not have exaggerated her ability with any description. Simply, she was superb. She was so into what she was doing that Julie felt she could have spoken and Rikki would not even have known she had said anything, she was so involved in Julie's cunt.

Julie was sighing softly, sucking in her breath, moaning. The wetness of her pussy was soaking right through her whole body. Her belly was heavy with the buildup of sex inside her, her legs were weak. Being eaten while standing up was always an astonishing sensation for her, and even more so now while juice and saliva, hot and fierce as burning oil, trickled down the inside of her naked thighs. She was a well of pussynectar, being tapped and then emptied by Rikki's fabulous tongue.

Rikki was moving faster now. With her hands, she indicated that Julie should move her legs apart. Julie did, until she was standing spread as wide as she could. Rikki knelt up under her, between her feet, so that her face was directly below Julie's cunt. From this position, she reached up so that she could stick her tongue into Julie's hole.

The heat and wetness was unbelievable. Julie felt as if Rikki's tongue was going to snake its way up right into her womb. Her tongue was as long and thin as she was: lithe, graceful, able to go wherever it wanted with a mind of its own. She rimmed the opening, went up deep inside it. She slipped back to tickle at Julie's asshole and then pushed the tip inside that forbidden muscular ring. The fullness of it left Julie gasping.

When Rikki came back in front of her, her lips and chin were shiny with juice. She licked it away, savoring it, but did not say a word; she simply went back to Julie's labia. She blew on it, gently, to cool it, and then listened to Julie gasp as she reapplied her hot tongue to warm it back up again. She was a delicate tease, knowing exactly what to do to bring out the most emotion in her new lover, and she played it to the hilt. She kept Julie right on the edge, undecided between buildup and coming, for the better part of half an hour. She had the ability to know just when Julie was close to coming, and then back away, letting her calm down before returning with her exquisite tongue to lick and lap again.

Julie was heady. It was so sweet to come so close, to back away, to come close again. It was a technique that Andrea had used many, many times on her, and in that way it was familiar. But it had never been like this, in this hot, cramped apartment, her panties around her feet, with this half-clothed stranger kneeling before her to give her this pleasure. She felt deliciously dirty. She also felt more alive than she thought she had ever felt before.

Then Rikki was right on her clit. It was fierce and soft at the same time, hot and wet, and Julie moaned as she felt her whole body rush into a knot at her pussy. It tightened and drew her even closer. Then it released, in a flood, and she could barely hold herself upright as she trembled and groaned. Rikki stayed with her until the very last tremors passed, sucking her juice in greedily.

When it was over, Julie stood, breathing hard, trying to calm herself. Rikki got up. Her face was wet with pussyjuice, and she wiped her chin on the back of her hand. She didn't say a word, and neither did Julie. Their eyes met and the flicker of a smile passed between them, but that was all.

Rikki walked over and lay down on the bed, her shorts and boots still on. Her tattoos were almost luminescent in their brilliant colors. She molded the pillow around her face and pulled the top sheet over herself, still without removing the rest of her clothes. Julie looked at her.

"I sleep alone," Rikki said, not unkindly. But there was no room for discussion in her tone, so Julie looked away and began to dress. Her clothes had been folded so neatly that there was not a wrinkle in them.

She was about to turn for the door when Rikki said, "You won't get a cab on this street this late at night. You go downstairs. I'll call one for you."

"Thank you," Julie said, but there was no reply. Without looking at Rikki again, she turned and left. When the door clicked shut behind her she almost wondered for a moment if she had dreamed the whole thing.

The hallway was cool and she wiped the thin film of sweat from her forehead as she walked down the stairs. She was surprised at herself; surprised that she had so willingly played the bottom, surprised that she had not been offended by Rikki's curt, domineering manner. But, more than anything, she was surprised at how completely satisfied she felt.

The cab took only a few minutes; when she opened the door, she found that the driver was a good-looking young woman. She gave her destination, and the car drove away from the curb.

The streets were empty in this part of the city; as they got closer to the area where Julie's hotel was, there were more and more people out. She hadn't really realized just where she had gone with Rikki. She caught the driver's eye in the rearview mirror and once again thought to herself that the cabbie must be wondering about her. Dressed as she was, going to such a fine hotel, but picked up at such an address. Indeed, it must be odd.

The cabdriver initiated the conversation. "Still a lot of people up at this hour," she said, testing the waters.

"I'm always surprised myself," Julie said.

"You're not from around here?"

Julie looked at the driver's picture card; her name was Nita. "I'm here for a few days," she said.

Nita was silent for a moment, and then said, "You know someone where I picked you up?"

"Yes." Julie wondered where this was going. "Why do you ask?"

Nita sounded almost shy. "I know someone there. A woman, lives alone. Her name is Rikki."

Julie's eyes flew to the mirror; they were stopped at a light, and she wasn't surprised to see Nita staring back at her. Julie hesitated for just a moment and then said, "I know her, too."

Neither of them said a word until they got to the hotel, although occasionally one or the other would look to the mirror and catch the other's eye. As satisfied as she had been before, Julie found herself becoming horny all over again. The coincidence was just too much, she told herself; she couldn't possibly have let it go.

Nita stopped the meter and waited for her money, as the doorman came out to open the door. With a gesture she told him to wait. Again she looked in the mirror, and again she caught Nita's glance. "I have the money for the meter," she said. "But if you'd like a tip, I'd have to go upstairs for it."

Nita smiled, and Julie could tell that she had been waiting for it. "I suppose I'd have to come up with you," she said.

"I'll wait in the lobby," Julie said and motioned to the doorman that she was ready. Once inside the glass doors, she watched as Nita pulled the car up to the taxi stand just off to the side of the lobby. She got out, explaining to the doorman that she had to collect her fare and that she would be back shortly. The doorman graciously held the heavy glass door open for her as well.

They passed Linda's room on the way to Julie's, and the editor looked over at it even as she was opening her own, Nita right behind her. All in good time, she told herself again, as she turned on the lights in her comfortable suite. But in the meantime, there's nothing wrong with times being good for me.

"INTRODUCTIONS"
(from *A Circle of Friends*)

"I've never done anything like this before," Laura said shyly.

"There's always a first time for everything," Janice told her confidently.

The music in the background, probably from the stereo on the shelf, was instrumental, with a heavy beat. Janice reached up to lift the silk shirt gently off Laura's shoulders. Underneath, Laura was wearing a wickedly sexy corset, red satin with black lace trim, not at all in keeping with her demure hesitation. It showed off her magnificent tits, pushed up over the wire foundation of the bra until the nipples were exposed. When Janice helped her off with her skirt, she was wearing only a tiny G-string under it, a scrap of black fabric that went enticingly up the crack of her firm, smooth ass, a G-string which they both worked to remove. She left on her high-heeled shoes and the corset, arranged her hair down over her shoulders, and licked her lips.

Janice kissed her, at first gently and then with a growing passion. Laura met her kisses and moaned as she felt the first touch of Janice's fingers brushing against her exposed pink nipples. Laura laid back on the pillow and Janice took off her own clothes. Under her business suit she also wore exotic lingerie, which she left on along with her high-heeled shoes. It was an outfit which left her crotch bare, and Laura reached out as if she wanted to touch it. "You have such a beautiful pussy," she said.

"Yours is lovely, too," Janice said. "It's all wet. See, you've wanted a woman all along." Then she kneeled on the bed and took Laura's tit into her mouth.

"It isn't so bad, is it?" she asked.

"No," Laura gasped. "It's better than I thought it would be. Oh, eat my cunt, Janice, I can't wait to have a woman there!"

Janice obliged immediately. She closed her eyes and sighed happily as she put her mouth to Laura's pussy and buried her face in it. Her fingers went between her own legs to manipulate her clit, her pussylips shining with her thick sweet fluid, as she licked her companion with a fierce ambition.

"It's so good!" Laura sighed, and began to roll her own nipples between her fingers. She was moaning almost constantly and every now and again she lifted her head off the pillow, looked down at Janice, and then threw her head back wildly and groaned some more. Janice arranged her hair behind her head and fell back to licking, stopping only to insert two fingers into Janice's pussy and move them slowly in and out.

"More! More!" Laura gasped—and then the screen went dark when Nora Stevens hit the button on the remote control to move the videotape to another scene.

She sighed and slumped into the corner of the sofa, watching the counter spin rapidly on the television screen. This particular film had a pretty corny plot, but some of the sex scenes were very hot and best of all, it was all women.

Nora loved watching women make love. She loved watching them on videotape and she loved looking at photos in magazines. She loved reading about women loving women. The thought of having a woman kiss her and make love to her, of putting her tongue to a woman's soft pussy and licking and sucking until she came, made her incredibly hot and wet between her legs. The only problem was that it was only a fantasy.

She stopped the tape, watched it for a moment, and then hit the fast-forward again. She was very horny and she wanted to make herself come, but she also wanted to do it while watching her favorite episode on this particular tape.

She thought about women while she watched the actresses on the screen go through their motions at the wildly exaggerated pace dictated by the speed of the tape. No other kind of sex appealed to her the way lesbian sex did, and nothing else made her as excited. The problem was that while she desperately wanted to satisfy this craving, she hadn't a clue as to how to go about doing it.

Finding men who were outspokenly attracted to her slim figure, her blonde hair, her nicely sized tits, and her radiantly blue eyes was relatively easy, but finding women who came on to her wasn't quite the same thing. She thought about going to a gay bar, but she didn't know of any, and didn't know anyone she could ask. Each day she read the personals column of her local newspaper, her eyes searching the page until she found the "Women Seeking Women" section. She read every ad completely through, surprised at the large number that appeared in each edition. Each day she made a mental game of it, shopping through them, eliminating the ones outside of her age range, choosing between the ones that appealed to her, until she finally found one that she thought she would like to answer.

She never did, although she did come so close that she actually picked up the phone and dialed one of the numbers, her heart pounding like a jackhammer, but she hung up after it rang twice. She wanted it desperately, but she was just too nervous to go through with it.

She wasn't even sure if she'd recognize a come-on if she received one—in fact, she wasn't even sure she knew what a lesbian looked like! She knew the movies she watched were nothing but voyeur fantasies acted out by actresses, and she knew that the film stereotype of the woman with teased blonde hair and blue-shadowed eyes—who kept her high-heeled shoes on in bed!—was just that. But did real lesbians look like she did, like the close-cropped women she saw on magazine covers, like the activists that marched in the Gay Pride parades? How would she know if a woman standing in front of her wanted Nora as much as Nora wanted her?

She thought she had been approached, but it was too subtle for her to be sure, and of course there was no way she could possibly ask what the woman's intentions were! Nora was a book illustrator and several times she had done work for an advertising agency where she always dealt with a woman named Charlotte West. She'd heard rumors that Charlotte was gay, that she was even married to another woman, but the stories had never been substantiated. Still, she felt like Charlotte had looked her up and down the way the men did, and once she had invited Nora to come out for a drink after work. Nora had had a deadline that day and had to refuse. The job almost didn't get done on time, for instead of concentrating on her work, Nora could only think about the possibilities, wondering beyond hope if the request for a drink had been just that or if she had been approached for something more. The fantasy that ran through her mind was so strong that she had to stop halfway through and obtain relief for her throbbing pussy with her fingers.

The tape counter reached the number she had been looking for, and she pressed the button to run the tape at normal speed. On the screen, two women returned to their hotel room after shopping, one of them complaining about how horny she was. Within moments, both were completely nude with their arms around each other.

Nora reached into the drawer of the table beside her and drew out a vibrator. Her eyes never leaving the screen, she pulled up the caftan she wore, revealing her blonde pussy. She was always amazed at how hot this particular scene made her, and without turning the vibrator on she rubbed it over her clit, shivering gently as she did so.

It was obvious the women were enjoying what they were doing, for they made love with a relish, giggling like schoolgirls at the joy of having each other. Nora was envious of them, and imagined herself beside them, turning a couple into a threesome. She wanted to touch the dark woman's breasts just as the redheaded woman was doing. She wanted to feel the warmth and the fullness with her fingers.

She turned the dial of the vibrator just a little, so that the plastic device buzzed gently against her sex-swollen clit. She liked to move it slowly, to build up to a dazzling climax just as the women on the screen came themselves. She had done it so many times to this particular tape that it was as carefully chore-ographed as a dance, and just as beautiful and satisfying. "Let me lick your pussy," the redhead said on the screen, and Nora whispered "Yes, yes, please!" even though she was barely aware that she did so. All she wanted was that dark woman's crotch next to her face, so that she could stretch out a probing tongue and lick the wetness away from the full lips, then stretch them wide and apply herself to that huge nub that waited inside for attention.

The women on the screen arranged themselves on the bed, the tall, dark woman on her back, the smaller redheaded woman settling herself over her. They were now cunt-to-mouth, and Nora sighed, for there was nothing she found as hot as a sixty-nine, and the camera made the most of this one. The vibrator was turned up a couple of notches, and she gasped as it sent thrills through her whole body from that hot, wet place between her legs.

The redhead's tongue probed at the darker woman's pussy, which had been shaved except for a small patch at the rise of her belly. Her cunt was naked, shining with the juices of her wanting, and Nora could see everything as the woman on top reached down with her tongue.

The tip of it seemed to slide into the triangle of her pussylips and almost disappear inside as it swept over the huge clit. Nora shivered. She wanted someone's tongue to touch her like that, and she longed to be able to part someone else's pussylips with hers and give them the thrill that she knew she could.

She didn't even realize she had stuck her own tongue out, as she moved the vibrator faster over her aching slit. She reached with it, as if she was licking upwards as the darker woman was doing, pulling her lover's asscheeks down so that she could bury her face in female flesh. Nora moaned and pulled the vibrator hard into her. When the camera showed both women, writhing and moaning, she turned it up as far as it would go and held it firmly against her clit.

Her whole body shook convulsively as she came, and she threw back her head and cried out loud as she did. When she was finished, she put the vibrator to her lips and licked the rich hot juice from it. She loved the taste of her own pussy, and she wondered if she would ever have the chance to taste another.

The next afternoon, she was invited again to have a drink with Charlotte West. Her heart pounding, her mouth dry, she whispered yes.

"This is Robin Smythe," Charlotte said. "I don't believe you've met."

Nora stood up from her chair and shook Robin's hand. She was still a little nervous—although a bit less now that she had finished her first drink—but now her main emotion was disappointment. If she had suspected even slightly that Charlotte was coming on to her, if she had hoped against hope that something might happen, the presence of this beautiful, tall, slim black woman, obviously invited to the bar by Charlotte, dispelled any chance of anything happening.

"I understand you're an illustrator," Robin said.

"I do books, yes," Nora said, as she accepted her second drink. "Recently I've been doing drawings for magazine advertisements as well, and that's how I met Charlotte. And you?"

"I have a clothing store," Robin said.

Nora sipped her drink. "Is that how you know Charlotte? She shops at your store?"

She couldn't miss the questioning look that Robin gave Charlotte, and she was confused. Had she said something wrong?

"Robin and I live together," Charlotte said. "I'm sorry, I thought you knew."

"Oh, roommates," Nora said. "I shared a house that way in college. It certainly kept the costs down."

"No," Charlotte said. "We're not roommates, we're lovers."

For a moment Nora didn't know what to say. It was a bit of a shock—she hadn't believed she'd ever meet real lesbians after all her years of watching her fantasies on screen. At the same time, she couldn't believe her fortune.

"I hope it doesn't shock you," Robin said.

"Oh—of course not," Nora said. Then, just a little giddy from the news and her drink, she blurted, "I always wanted to meet someone like you." She couldn't believe she had said it, but at the same time, she saw the look that passed between the two women. She drew in her breath as their eyes met.

They sat for the longest time, making small talk until Nora thought that she would explode. Finally she could hold it no longer, and she said, "Charlotte,

I appreciate your thoughtfulness, and I'm enjoying myself very much, but why did the two of you ask me to come for a drink?"

The two women looked at each other for several seconds, until finally Robin leaned forward and said quietly, "We thought you might like to come up for a nightcap later. At our house."

Nora was almost in a daze as they finished their drinks and Charlotte got a cab for them. Even when she was sitting in their living room, being offered a snifter of finest brandy, she still felt as if she were watching a movie of three other people sitting and talking. It was just too hard to believe that it was really happening to her.

She was still in this dreamy state when Charlotte came over to sit beside her, and she felt a hand on her leg, moving slowly and smoothly to caress her thigh. Charlotte's voice was warm and low in her ear. "We thought you might be the sort of woman for this," she said. "Were we correct? Is this what you want too?"

Nora smiled, and it only seemed real when she put her hand down and set it over Charlotte's warm fingers. "I've never done this before," she admitted.

Charlotte withdrew her hand, and apologized, but Nora, shocked at her own forthrightness, reached over and took the hand, putting it back on her own leg. "No, please," she said, looking at both of them. "I've never done this, but I want to, please! This is what I've always wanted, always!"

The two women looked at each other again, and Nora immediately understood the unspoken language they shared, as Robin came over to sit beside her and take her brandy glass away. It was still happening as if in a dream, for it was almost beyond comprehension that after all those years of watching videos and wishing, it was finally going to happen.

She hardly even felt the buttons of her shirt being opened, but she definitely knew when Charlotte's fingers found her breasts and stroked them as softly as a whisper. Her whole body reacted to it, and she looked down and saw her nipples standing out, hard and wanting. The sight of Robin's dark skin on hers was rich and comforting, lovely to look at. She leaned back into the sofa and let the two women feel her breasts. The warmth that went through her whole body was almost indescribable.

They undressed her slowly, running their hands over her long legs and commenting on the blondness of her sweet cunt.

Then Charlotte took her hand and helped her up off the sofa. "Come in the bedroom, it's much more comfortable," she said. Robin was slowly running her hands over Nora's back, cupping the tight swell of her asscheeks. "I remember my first time. I want it to be as nice for you."

The bedroom was quite different from what Nora was expecting as well. In all the movies she had seen, the bedrooms were usually either overdone or just a bed on a cheap set. The room that Charlotte and Robin shared was very tastefully decorated, the furniture heavy and well made, the bed inviting with fluffy pillows and a spotless white duvet. The feather comforter was warm and gently yielding as she sat down on it.

The women undressed each other in front of her and then sat down on either side of her, naked. Nora couldn't help but stare at them. She was intrigued by

Charlotte's delicious tits, by the wiry dark hair on Robin's pussy. She wanted to touch them both so badly that her very fingers felt hungry for them, but even though she was sitting completely undressed between them, she was too shy.

"You say you've never had a woman before," Robin said. "How do you know that you want us?"

Nora loved the look of her dark nipples. "I've always wanted a woman, as long as I can remember," she said. "I watch women in movies and I want to touch them and lick them. I've wanted it so badly that I can't believe this is happening."

"Believe it," Robin said, and put her lips to Nora's and kissed her hard. It was the first of many touches Nora had been waiting for. Robin's lips were soft and full and so delightfully warm against hers, and when she pressed her tongue to Nora, the blonde woman took it and met it with her own. As she kissed Robin, a long lingering one that Nora thought might never end, Charlotte was reaching over to caress her body. The touch of the brunette woman's hands on her arms, on her shoulders, teasing her nipples, was amazing.

"I can hardly wait to taste you," she begged when Robin finally leaned back.

"There's time enough for everything," the black woman said. "I don't know about you, but we have all night."

"All night's just fine with me," Nora said, and she submitted to the pressure of Charlotte's hands inviting her to lie back on the bed.

She was still a bit nervous, and the two women spent a long time helping her to relax. They ran their hands all over her, giving as much time to her arms and legs as they did to her breasts and the thin, light hair that adorned her pussy, until she lay back, soaking it all up and moaning softly at the touch of their fingers. Finally Robin leaned down and parted her legs gently, then flicked her tongue against Nora's hard, aching clit.

Nora's whole body trembled at the touch and she moaned out loud. She had had her clit touched many times before, as often as not by her own hand or her vibrator, and each time it was a delightful rush throughout her whole body. But when she looked down and saw Robin's face between her legs, licking her, while Charlotte's hands played with her tits, it was as if she was a virgin experiencing sex for the first time in her life. Never had anything felt so good.

Robin moved very slowly over Nora's cunt, licking everything she possibly could. She ran her tongue into the place where Nora's legs curved into the sides of her pussy, and up her thighs. She moved down to lick at Nora's tight ass, pulling her cheeks gently apart with her hands and kneading them with her fingers as she did. She made long laps on Nora's vaginal lips, and made a point of her tongue so that she could slip the tip of it into the entrance to Nora's hot, soaking tunnel. Everything she did seemed to feel better than the last, and Nora moaned loudly.

"Would you like to try me now?" Charlotte whispered, and Nora nodded. She didn't even realize that the tip of her own tongue was pushed between her lips, as it always was when she watched the films on television, longing to touch it to female flesh. She didn't even trust her voice when Charlotte asked; it was enough that her fantasy was coming true.

Charlotte climbed up on the bed and knelt over Nora's face. At first, Nora did nothing but stare and breathe deeply. She couldn't get over how beautiful Charlotte's cunt was and how good it smelled, so hot and ready, so in need of a tongue to relieve the pressure built up inside. No movie or photo had come even close to capturing the reality of Charlotte's pussy suspended so close over her face. Before she even touched it, she knew that this was going to be a rare experience, one that lived up to the expectations of her fantasy.

Hardly daring to breathe, she reached up and held Charlotte's strong thighs with her hands and pulled that gorgeous pussy down so that she could reach it with her mouth. She touched it with her tongue. The taste was delicious and she savored it, the heat was almost unbelievable. Charlotte didn't rush her, but was content to hold herself there, enjoying the feeling as Nora's tongue touched her at first shyly, then with growing confidence and desire. Now it was time for Charlotte to move on Nora's tongue, and she did, slowly, sensually, reaching down with her hands to hold Nora's tits and massage the nipples between her fingers.

"It looks so good from here," Charlotte said. Robin smiled up at her, then went back to sucking Nora's blonde pussy. "Nora, your tongue feels great on my cunt," Charlotte continued. "That's it, that's my clit. Lick it, lick it hard! Just like that!"

Nora needed no encouragement at this point. She didn't think her tongue could move that fast, but Charlotte's obvious enjoyment, combined with the effect that Robin was having on her cunt, was driving her wild. She found the hard nub of Charlotte's clit and homed in on it. It felt deliciously hot and wet on her tongue, slippery from the sweet juice of Charlotte's pussy. The taste and the heat were better than she had ever imagined in her wildest fantasies. She pulled Charlotte close to her, and when Charlotte ground her pussy against Nora's tongue, the blonde woman went almost crazy with desire for more.

This was what she was meant to do! The black woman's mouth on her cunt was thrilling her, but having her own tongue on another's clit was just as exciting. Her tits felt deliciously full, almost throbbing, at the touch of Charlotte's hands on them. She was close to coming, but her two lovers realized it, and when they moved away from her, she gasped and moaned.

"Take it easy," Robin whispered to her, as she moved up from between Nora's thighs to lie on top of her and softly kiss her. "We have the whole night to ourselves. This is only the beginning." She mashed her tits into Nora's, and Charlotte used her fingers to feel both of the women, the rich dark brown tits and the pale white ones, their nipples touching, turning each other on.

After several more sensual kisses, Robin got up, and she and Charlotte had Nora stand up. They spent a long time running their hands over her, and Nora groaned as she felt Charlotte's fingers part her pussylips and slowly rub the clit between them, so desirous and so close to coming that she felt weak. When Charlotte finally took her hand away, she put it to Nora's mouth, and Nora was rewarded with the taste of her own steamy pussy on Charlotte's fingers. She sucked them eagerly, slipping her own hand between Charlotte's legs to touch her there. It felt as natural as anything she could imagine, and it only turned her on more when Robin insisted on licking the thick, sweet nectar from her hand. Then the black woman kissed her, and when she probed with her tongue, they shared the pussyjuice together in their mouths, moaning softly, their cunts on fire.

Now the two women knelt on the floor beside Nora, Charlotte in front of her and Robin behind, and gently they positioned her feet so that her thighs were apart, her slit bared to them. Each took her place. Charlotte licked at Nora's pussy, while Robin used her fingers and her tongue to explore the hot rosebud of Nora's ass. Even though Robin had licked her there before, Nora was still new to the experience and a bit hesitant. She clenched her muscles at the first touch of Robin's tongue, but when she forced herself to relax, she realized that it was unlike anything she had ever enjoyed before, hot and delightfully wicked, and within moments she was begging Robin to explore deeper.

Both Charlotte and Robin were eager to respond to her plea, and they licked at her with a renewed passion, fueled by the fact that they had reached under her and had their hands in each other's cunts even as they gave pleasure to the third woman between them. When Nora saw this she put her head back and moaned out loud. While the reality had finally hit her—the fact that it was true, that two beautiful women were making love to her and she to them!—it was still the culmination of her fantasy, and she was drinking in every moment of it. She could almost feel the hot, slick juice on her fingers, and she could see Robin's dark hand shine with the sweet liquid from Charlotte's crotch.

They were bathing her with their tongues, exploring every crevice, and when Charlotte slipped two fingers into Nora's soaked hole, she was filled completely. Fingers in her ass, fingers in her cunt, tongues exploring and licking, harder, stronger, faster, and then she came, her whole body going hot as fire, the orgasm racing through her and leaving her breathless.

She had to sit on the bed, afraid that she might collapse, for her bones had all but melted away. Charlotte and Robin were on her in a moment, prolonging the ecstasy by caressing every inch of her body with their hands. When she could finally speak again, Nora asked them if they would fulfill another fantasy of hers. They did, moving into a sixty-nine on the bed, cunt to mouth, pink flesh to pink tongues, while Nora sat and watched them in this, her favorite position. Inhibitions completely gone now, she even reached over and touched Robin's sweet ass with her own fingers. Unable to stop herself, spurred on by Robin's moans, she slipped her finger inside, amazed at the heat of this orifice, completely turned on by the fact that she was inside a woman being eaten by another. When they came, it was as if her own body was convulsing again, trembling with the heat of a climax.

After a long while, they slipped beneath the comforter, and Nora relaxed in their arms, warm under the duvet, held on both sides by women. Their skin was softer than she could imagine, and she loved the feeling of their nipples up against her, their flat bellies and their hairy mounds pressed tight against her.

And when Charlotte leaned over to brush her cunt, she responded in turn. Feeling another woman's pussy was no longer a fantasy, but the most natural thing in the world.

"HARDEST LESSONS"
(from *Bad Habits*)

When dominatrix Wendy Hudson discovered how badly trained her submissive was, and when other dominatrixes complained of the same problem, she decided to open a "school for slaves," with herself as teacher, to educate them properly. Most learned eagerly, but the beautiful and headstrong Margot refused to respond to her lessons. Wendy accepted this as a most interesting challenge.

"**M**istress, please!" Alicia begged. "No, Mistress! Please have mercy!"

"I am merciful, worm," Wendy replied. "I could have chained you upside down."

Alicia sobbed. She stood spread-eagled, chained by her wrists and ankles to the X-frame against the wall.

Her bare back was exposed to her teacher, who stepped behind her with a varnished wooden paddle in her hand.

The other four students were kneeling on the floor, watching; Margot's eyes were bright with anticipation. Alicia had committed the grievous error of being one minute late for class.

"This will be a lesson to all of you," Wendy said. She walked back and forth between the students on the floor and the black-haired woman chained to the frame, her shoes tapping a warning on the hard wood. Her costume this day was a body-hugging catsuit made of supple black leather. "Punctuality is one of the most important things a slave must learn. If she is not punctual, she is not obedient. If she is not obedient, then she will never be a perfect slave."

She reached over and ran the wooden paddle down Alicia's spine and into the crack of her delicate ass. Alicia held her breath. When the paddle was removed, she let out a sob.

"Imagine this picture," Wendy said. "Your mistress tells you to meet her outside a restaurant at five o'clock. You don't arrive until a quarter past. Your mistress stands outside for fifteen minutes waiting for you. She looks foolish hanging around outside a restaurant waiting. People wait for her, she doesn't wait for them! Would you put your mistress in such a situation?"

She waited; the slaves were silent. Wendy whacked the paddle against her palm with a loud crack. "Would you?" she demanded.

"No, Mistress!" the class chimed.

"Late is late," Wendy said. "Whether it's one minute or fifteen, it's still disobedience. And it will not be tolerated!"

Thwack! The wooden paddle landed on Alicia's buttocks. She cried out, and the other slaves winced. The long, thin paddle left a stunning welt across both asscheeks. Wendy smiled with satisfaction.

"If your mistress tells you to arrive at five, you arrive at five o'clock," Wendy continued. "You are not early, you are not late. You are precisely punctual."

Thwack! Another welt joined the first on Alicia's creamy asscheeks. Her face was wet with tears and she slumped against the frame, held up by the shackles on her wrists.

"You do not try to outthink your mistress, and you do not try to anticipate her," Wendy continued. "You do exactly what you are told. If she says five o'clock, you are there at exactly five o'clock. If you know she is going to be late, you are there at five o'clock, and you wait for her. There is no other way to behave."

Thwack! Thwack! The blows came quickly together, and Alicia gritted her teeth and squeezed her eyes shut to keep from screaming out. Her ass was burning and blood red.

"That looks so nice," Wendy said, standing back and admiring her handiwork. "I hope this is an effective lesson for all of you. If anyone is late for any other class, she will not graduate. Period." Thwack! "She will not participate in the graduation ceremony, and she will not receive her graduation honor." Thwack! "She will have to repeat her lessons, and be shamed before all of her classmates and her mistress." Wendy held the paddle with both hands now, and delivered a final, terrifyingly hard blow to Alicia's ass. Alicia screamed, then sobbed loudly as her poor bruised ass welled up an angry red in response.

Wendy put the paddle down and went back to the

front of the classroom. "Does everyone understand?" she asked.

"Yes, Mistress," the class replied.

"I would suggest that before you leave today, you ensure that your watches are synchronized with the clock here," she said, ignoring Alicia's loud sobs. "It might help you avoid the situation your poor sister has gotten herself into."

Wendy then went on with her regular lesson, teaching the slaves how to make and serve coffee. She noticed that every now and again, Margot stole a quick glance over at Alicia as she hung on the X-frame, her buttocks raw and burning. Wendy couldn't mistake the look in Margot's eyes, and she knew that the tall gorgeous slave longed to be paddled herself.

"Margot," Wendy said, "perhaps you'd like to demonstrate to the rest of the class how to set the tray for coffee."

Margot paused just a moment before she replied, "Yes, Mistress," and Wendy knew that she was eager for her share of punishment. She was definitely jealous that Alicia had received such cruel fare and when she got up, she walked slowly. From the corner of her eye, she watched Wendy to see if her tardiness was having any effect.

If it was, Wendy didn't let it show. She played Margot as she had before, teasing her with a promise of pain and then holding back. She picked up a riding crop and used it to gently tap Margot's hand, explaining that she should pick up the cup by the handle. Margot left her hand on the cup for a moment longer, then realized that there would be no further blows from the crop. Disappointed, she handled the cup properly and put it on the tray.

"The napkin must be folded properly," Wendy said, and the class watched as Margot folded it. The spoon was placed incorrectly, but again to her disappointment, Margot received only a slight tap with the riding crop as a warning.

The rest of the class looked on, wondering why Wendy wasn't beating this slave senseless. A sharp glance from their mistress immediately let them know that such behavior would be tolerated from no one else. Kneeling on her heels, Brenda got the impression that the only person in the room who didn't realize a plan was brewing was Margot herself. The tall slave seemed oblivious to the fact that she was being set up for a terrible and final punishment. Brenda shivered involuntarily as she thought about what was going through her mistress' mind, and she was only grateful that her mistress' wrath would not be aimed at her.

The class watched as Margot poured the coffee into the cup and set it on the tray, then carried it over to Wendy and presented it.

"I trust everyone watched carefully," Wendy said, ignoring Margot who stood before her. Wendy then walked to the front of the class, leaving Margot standing foolishly in the middle of the room with the tray in her hands. Wendy watched from the corner of her eye.

Margot stood for a moment, almost in disbelief. She looked over at Wendy, who was now explaining the finer points of cappuccino to Brenda, Leslie and Ellen. She completely ignored Margot, whose face turned red. For a moment, Wendy thought that she might fling the tray to the floor. Instead, she stood for a long moment, then humbly brought the tray back to the front of the class. Still ignored by her mistress, she returned the tray to the table and then took her place beside the other three.

Another victory! Wendy thought triumphantly. Her plan was working, and the other slaves knew it too. It would only be a matter of time, and a few more events, before Margot would become the magnificent, perfectly trained slave that Wendy knew she could be. Leah was right; the slut was worth the trouble. Besides, Wendy was rather enjoying the cat-and-mouse game she was playing. The best part was that Margot seemed to be completely oblivious to it. The final showdown, Wendy knew, would be terrifying and also immensely satisfying. She was actually looking forward to it, even though an exact plan was still in the future.

Once they had gone over espresso and iced coffee, Wendy walked over to the wall and released the shackles on Alicia's wrists.

The young slave gasped in agony as the feeling came back into her numb hands as a prickly fire. She did not forget her training, however, and managed to sob, "Thank you, Mistress!" as she rubbed her chafed wrists. Her poor ass was still throbbing, colored a rich burgundy from the wooden paddle. Wendy noted that it would probably be a few days before she would be able to sit comfortably.

Wendy opened the cuffs that held her legs apart, then ordered Alicia over with the rest of the class. "Thank you, Mistress," Alicia repeated, as she hurried over to her place in line and knelt on the floor. Wendy noticed that while all the others sat on their heels, Alicia was careful to keep her asscheeks up so that the burnished skin would not be touched.

Wendy also noticed that Margot kept glancing over

at Alicia. The fact that Alicia could not put her ass down was not lost on the tall, cold slave. Wendy decided that it was time to put Margot's longing for pain to good use. Although she hadn't planned on using this particular lesson just yet, it seemed like perfect timing. Not only would the other slaves benefit, but she would have an opportunity to win yet another victory over Leah's belligerent slave.

"You may recall," Wendy said, stepping to the front of the class, "that a little while ago, you were taught how to properly present yourselves when your mistress wanted to secure you. I believe we used such items as thumbscrews and handcuffs, did we not?"

"Yes, Mistress," the class chimed, and Wendy noticed that there was no hesitation on Margot's part when she answered.

"It's very important that your education be complete," Wendy continued. "The restraints we learned about the last time were very basic ones. It's time to move on to other things."

Margot's eyes went as bright as Christmas candles. As Wendy left the room, she saw that the tall slave followed her every move. When she returned, carrying a large bag, Margot looked like a child who had been promised candy. Keep falling, little one, Wendy thought. The trap is set and you're walking straight into it.

The first item Wendy pulled out of the bag was a bridle, her most recent acquisition from Julie's store. At the center was a cold steel snaffle bit, the same type that a horse would wear. The difference was that the leather bridle attached to it was shaped to go over a woman's head. There were long reins attached to the bit rings.

"Margot, come up here," Wendy ordered, and she marveled at how quickly Margot got up and rushed to the front of the classroom. Very soon, she thought, you'll be doing that for every command I give.

"The bridle is an important toy for a mistress," Wendy explained, holding it up. Margot's eyes never left it. "It can be used for riding a slave or for guiding her. It also makes a very good gag. Leslie, come up here."

Leslie did; Margot looked confused. Wendy turned to her. "Margot, put the bridle on Leslie," she said. "I think it's fairly obvious how it goes on."

Margot's face fell. She stood for a second, then replied, "Yes, Mistress," and unbuckled the straps to the bridle.

Leslie was totally unaware of Margot's disappointment; she was too excited by the bridle. As a novice, she had never seen such a thing, and she loved it. All the glasses of wine served, all the taps with the riding crop she had endured—now this was a reward! She could not believe how wet the device was making her pussy. She wanted to wear it for Mistress Wendy, and she longed to be buckled into it by her own beloved Mistress Anne.

She opened her mouth wide; Margot roughly shoved the bit in. The steel was cold on Leslie's tongue and it pinched painfully where the rings came out at the sides of her mouth, but, to her delight, she found that she loved it! Margot buckled the straps around her head and the bridle was firmly in place.

"On your knees," Wendy ordered, and Leslie did so eagerly. Wendy picked up a riding crop and grabbed the long reins, standing behind Leslie. She tapped Leslie's ass with the crop as she would a horse in harness. "Forward," she ordered. Leslie moved ahead on her hands and knees.

"You will notice how your mistress will use the bridle to control you," Wendy told the class. They were learning about this new form of control. But their lessons were nothing compared to the revelation that Leslie herself was going through.

She moved forward on her hands and knees in front of Mistress Wendy. As she did, her face flushed and her heart began beating wildly. She was so excited, she thought she might come just from Wendy pulling her head to the side with the bit. The smell of the leather, the steely taste of the bit in her mouth, even the coppery sting of the drop of blood that appeared at the corner of her lip—all excited her even more. So this was what being a slave was all about!

She had been controlled by her mistress through commands and through the occasional punishment she had received. But nothing compared to this! Mistress Wendy had total control over her. She slowed for just a moment, and received a sharp crack of the riding crop across her ass. She moved just slightly in the wrong direction, and had her head pulled back immediately by the reins. She could go nowhere on her own, do nothing that she wanted to do. She was completely in Mistress Wendy's control, at Mistress Wendy's mercy. And she loved it!

Wendy led her back to the front of the class. "Your mistress will undoubtedly come up with many more uses for this kind of device," she said. "A slave can also be ridden, in addition to being driven." To illustrate, she sat on Leslie's naked back.

Leslie gasped with pleasure. The weight on her back, the feel of Wendy's supple leather catsuit on her skin, the way Wendy gathered up the reins and used the ends to whip her across the shoulders—she shuddered and tightened the muscles in her pussy in an effort to stop it from throbbing so much.

Wendy ordered her forward, and Leslie immediately obeyed. It was much more difficult with the extra weight on her back, and at one point a tiny piece of gravel tracked in on Wendy's shoes cut painfully into her knee. She didn't care. She would have carried Wendy on her back out on the street if her teacher had ordered it. The only thing that could have made her happier at this point was if Mistress Anne had been there. But she was confident that her beautiful mistress would use this kind of treatment in the future. She would beg on her belly if necessary, but she would find a way to be controlled!

For her part, Wendy didn't miss any of Leslie's revelation. She had noticed the look in Leslie's eyes, heard her gasp and, most importantly, had seen the glint of moisture around Leslie's exposed pussy. Wendy herself was so excited she could hardly believe it. She had succeeded! She knew exactly what Leslie was feeling at this point, and she knew why.

Wendy was so excited she could feel the crotch of her leather suit becoming hot and damp. She had taken an untrained, novice slave, who was so green she hardly even knew what slavery was all about, and had cultivated her from a tiny seed into a beautiful blossom.

Wendy rode Leslie around the room, and as ordered, the other slaves watched every move. One of them needed no orders to do so. Margot's mouth was positively watering as she watched. She glanced quickly into the large bag and saw a jumble of leather, chrome rings, and chains. She wondered what device she would be strapped into! Whatever it was, she would love it! She listened carefully as Wendy described how a slave should behave once she was strapped into the bridle. "Quite often you will be given a saddle to wear as well," she said, and both Margot and Leslie closed their eyes, letting a rush of sexual energy pass through them as they imagined the slap of the leather saddle as it was dropped on their backs and the heft of the metal stirrups slapping against their sides. Leslie longed for the feeling of the girth being tightened around her stomach, and she decided that as soon as she saw her Mistress Anne again, she would plead and beg for such treatment.

"Sometimes your mistress will even strap spurs on her boots," Wendy said, and Margot thought she might faint with the joy. Imagine the tips of blunt spurs against her ribs or, even better, a razor-sharp rowel! She could almost hear the jingle of the spurs and the ringing of their chains on the floor, how they would look against the black leather of a riding boot. Her mind wandered to Mistress Leah, dressed in chaps and pointed-toe boots, spurs on them, fringed leather gloves on her hands, a riding whip between her fingers, carrying the saddle and bridle. How she would obey her commands then! How quickly she would drop to the floor when ordered! How she would carry her mistress around, speed up at the tap of a whip or the touch of a spur, change course when her head was cruelly pulled around by the bit! Her thighs were wet with juice as she imagined the scene, and both she and Leslie were disappointed when horse and rider returned to the front of the class and that portion of the lesson was finished.

Swiftly, Wendy unbuckled the bridle and pulled the bit out from between Leslie's teeth. "Face the class," she ordered, and Leslie did so. "Sit down there," she told Margot, indicating her spot in the lineup. Slowly, Margot left her spot beside the bag of leather devices and reluctantly knelt on the floor.

"Class, I believe that something very important has happened here right now," Wendy told the class. She looked down at Leslie. "Am I correct, slave?"

Leslie smiled, and tears of joy appeared at the corners of her eyes. "Oh, mistress, you know!" she beamed. "I was hoping you would, Mistress!"

Wendy smiled at her. "Perhaps you will tell the class what we're talking about," she said.

Leslie faced her classmates. "Mistress Wendy is correct," she said. "Something did happen just now. When my own mistress enrolled me in this school, I didn't really know a lot about being a slave. I thought it just meant that I would bring my mistress her wine when she asked for it, and rub her back when she ordered it, and carry out her duties. I'm ashamed to admit it," she said, lowering her head a little, "for a while I wasn't really sure if it was what I wanted. It seemed pretty menial to me. I didn't really understand why the other slaves my mistress kept always looked so happy and were so eager to serve my mistress. I knew I had to be missing the point of it all, but I didn't know exactly what the point was."

"Go on," Wendy coaxed. "Tell them what happened."

"It all became clear to me when Mistress Wendy put the bridle on me, and forced me to obey her," Leslie continued. "I'd never been controlled so physically before. I haven't been with my mistress very long and she hasn't had the time to restrain me and force me the way Mistress Wendy just did. Now I know what being a slave is all about. I don't have any will at all of my own. I am my mistress' property, and I must do my mistress' bidding, whether it's a spoken command or a physical force. I am happy to say that I am a slave! And I am proud to be one!"

The other slaves on the floor broke into spontaneous applause. After a moment, they stopped and looked at Wendy, remembering their place. But Wendy smiled and nodded, and the applause continued—with the exception of Margot, who looked sullenly at the woman who had just found her calling.

"I think you should welcome Leslie into the fold," Wendy said, and as Wendy took her place, the others hugged and kissed her, congratulating her on her discovery. Then Leslie turned to her teacher, smiling. "Thank you, Mistress Wendy, thank you!" she cried. "I am forever in your debt, Mistress Wendy!"

"That will be enough," Wendy said, returning instantly to her role as teacher. The classroom instantly became quiet, all eyes on her. Their moment of gaiety, allowed by their teacher, was over. They were once again slaves.

"We will get on with our lesson," Wendy said, picking up her riding crop and using it to point at Brenda. "Up here, right now. And Margot, you come here as well."

Once again Margot was ordered to put a restraint on her fellow slave; this time, it was a cruel leather cone that was slipped over Brenda's head. It was big enough that it completely covered her torso, with only her head sticking out through the hole in the top. A strap was passed between her legs and buckled so that she was unable to move her arms at all. A second strap was tightened around the cone to hold her firmly.

"In this device," Wendy said, "your mistress can control you completely." She used her stiletto-heeled boot to push the kneeling slave over. Brenda could do nothing but fall on her side, unable to put out her hands to break her fall. Margot sucked in her breath quickly as she saw how helpless Brenda was. Why couldn't she be the one in the leather cone!

Wendy demonstrated a few more features of the cone, and showed how a mistress might open the straps to allow a bit of a movement, or tighten them completely so that a slave would not even be able to wiggle her fingers. Then, on Wendy's orders, Margot slowly unbuckled the straps and pulled the cone roughly over Brenda's head. Both of them returned to their places and knelt on the floor.

Wendy decided it was time for Margot to receive a little extra training. Since mild punishment was the reward that Margot so badly craved, Wendy thought that she would prove to the gorgeous slave that here no rewards were given out unless orders were obeyed, and obeyed immediately without question or hesitation. Since she was still hot and wet from riding Leslie around the room, Wendy thought that she might combine a little lesson with a bit of pleasure. She opened the metal snaps that held the crotch of her leather catsuit closed and pulled the flaps back. Her beautiful dark pussy was exposed, shiny with juice and throbbing with excitement.

She walked over to Margot, who knelt on the floor before her, and stood so that her pussy was right over the slave. "Pleasure me," she ordered.

Margot looked at her for a moment, then turned her head and said, "You're not my mistress."

The room was deathly silent, and then a loud collective gasp went up from the other four slaves. None of them could believe it. Their shock immediately turned to dread as they looked at Wendy's face.

Margot, too, was silent as she met Wendy's eyes. Her words, so carelessly thrown out, had doomed her and she knew it. Instantly she was on the floor, crying out, "Mistress, I'm sorry! Please forgive me, Mistress! I didn't know what I was saying! Please, Mistress, mercy!"

Wendy's controlled fury made her voice so cold that Alicia closed her eyes and tried to shrink away. "Too late for that, you stupid, worthless fuck," Wendy told Margot, who was on her belly on the floor. "I don't really think you understand just what kind of a predicament your mouth has gotten you into. I don't want to hear another word out of you until I order you to speak. By that time you will be grateful to obey every command any mistress ever gives you."

She reached down and wrapped her fist around Margot's heavy collar, then dragged her on the floor over to the wall. Although she struggled, Margot was no match for the powerful mistress and she could only sob as her spine bumped on the hard floor.

At the wall, Wendy selected the gruesome leather mask. Roughly she pulled it down over Margot's face and snapped it closed around her neck. Then once again she pulled the tall slave over the floor to the front of the class. Margot's sobs were muffled by the black leather as Wendy swiftly handcuffed her wrists together behind her back.

"I will never give a command that will not be

obeyed!" Wendy hissed. The other four slaves cringed, but Wendy ignored them completely. This was the turning point and they all knew it. Wendy would not stop this lesson now until Margot was completely, entirely broken.

"Stick your tongue out!" Wendy ordered, but Margot was sobbing too hard to obey. Ruthlessly Wendy picked up the riding crop and stuck the handle inside Margot's mouth. She pushed down on her tongue and forced her to stick it out. Then she pulled the zipper across. Margot's tongue stuck out of the side of the leather mouth. She couldn't pull it back in because the edges of the zipper bit into the tender side of her tongue; she had to leave it right where it was, stuck grotesquely out of the corner of the leather opening.

"I gave you an order, and you are going to carry it out!" Wendy said. She dragged Margot upright on her knees by the heavy leather collar. Then, with a hand on either side of the leather-clad head, Wendy pulled Margot against her pussy. Margot's tongue, pulled out and held tight by the mask's zipper, rubbed against her clit.

While the rest of the class watched, horrified and yet fascinated, Wendy used Margot's tongue like a dildo. Margot gasped and cried but was helpless as her tongue was rubbed against Wendy's hot, wet clit.

Wendy pleasured herself with the slave's tongue. To her delight she found it exciting. The domineering slave was now totally under her control! The thought made her pussy burn even more, and she cooled it with the tip of Margot's tongue. She pressed back and forth, pushing against her clit, ignoring Margot's sobs and concentrating on how good her pussy felt to have the unwilling tongue rubbed against it.

Her clit was throbbing with a life of its own. "Suck my pussy, scum!" she whispered, and roughly maneuvered Margot's head. Spreading her legs wide apart, she moved forward until Margot's tongue was on the entrance to her tunnel, then she pushed back so that the tip was pressing her clit. Hot rushes went through her body, born both of sex and dominance. It was the ultimate reward for a mistress—to humiliate completely, to dominate absolutely! It was Wendy's finest hour and she gloried in it.

"Never again will you deny a mistress!" she told Margot, as she pushed and pulled at the masked woman. "Never again will you disobey a command!"

She rubbed hard against her clit. The mask was now soaked with her pussy juice. Margot, in agony, was unable to do anything but submit to her mistress' whims. At one point she fell back on her heels, but Wendy grabbed her by the heavy collar and roughly pulled her back upright so that her tongue would once again reach Wendy's wet cunt.

She pushed Margot away for a moment and cried, "Will you disobey me again?" Unable to answer, Margot shook her head no. Immediately her swollen tongue, cramped in its position and cut by the cruel metal zipper, was pushed back against Wendy's clit. After a moment, she was pushed back again. "Will you obey your commands when they're given?" The leather mask nodded assent, and was again forced back to Wendy's cunt. "Have you learned your lesson?" More nodding, and again the rough push back to the swollen clit.

Wendy was now using Margot's tongue not to punish her, but to please herself. The most delicious sensations were running through her whole body as she rubbed her clit on Margot's tongue. A heady rush went though her and she trembled just a bit. Then her clit exploded and she ground Margot's head against her cunt as she went over the edge and came.

Once the last swell had died down, there was no basking in the afterglow. Immediately she grabbed Margot's collar and dragged her across the floor. The leather mask was shiny with a mixture of saliva, pussy juice and a bit of thin, watery blood from the cut on Margot's tongue. Still unable to pull her tongue back in because of the zipper's teeth, Margot was limp, her tongue sticking out foolishly from the side of the mouth. There was no fight left in her at all.

She was dragged to her feet before she even realized what was going on; then, roughly, Wendy shoved her into the leather sling that hung from the ceiling. Face down in the sling, Margot could only whimper and lie still. Her hands were still cuffed behind her back and she was completely at Wendy's mercy.

Wendy was anything but merciful. "There's something to be said for you, worm," Wendy said scornfully. "At least I'm getting a chance to try out all my new purchases." She went through the large bag and then walked back to the sling where Margot was held.

The first item was a pair of nipple clamps, but these were especially nasty ones. Attached to each clamp was a small, thin chain, and at the end of the chain was a small lead weight. Reaching under the sling, Wendy pulled Margot's nipples between the straps of the sling. Margot cried out as a clamp was snapped onto each nipple. The weights pulled them down, and the other four slaves winced as they saw Margot's breasts stretched out, the nipples held by the metal clasps.

The second object was even worse. It was a large purple dildo, long and thick, with a huge knobby head. Without any ceremony, Wendy spread Margot's asscheeks and jammed the dildo inside. Margot screamed, muffled by the leather mask.

Then, calmly, Wendy looked over her handiwork, smiled, and returned to the front of the class. The four slaves were as attentive as they could possibly be when, to their shock, Wendy casually went right back to the lesson she had been giving before Margot had given her such trouble. When ordered, Ellen stood at the front of the class, and Wendy demonstrated the proper way to stand when a slave was required to wear a leather device that chained her ankles to a collar around her throat.

All of them ignored the slave in the corner, Wendy because it was part of her plan, and the other students because they dared not turn around and look. It was difficult for them not to. Margot was anything but quiet about her agony. Occasionally she would sob hysterically, and then calm down to a whimper. Once she tried to squirm in the sling, but screamed when the nipple weights and the dildo in her ass moved. Wendy smiled to herself. Everyone has a breaking point, she thought. I finally found this one's.

The lesson went on for half an hour, then Wendy walked to the back of the room where Margot hung helpless. Because the leather mask covered her ears, Margot wasn't aware that Wendy was beside her. Wendy reached under the sling, grabbed the nipple weights, and yanked them off by their chains. Margot almost blacked out, and her muffled scream was so loud that the other slaves were chilled through. Alicia's hands went to her own nipples in sympathy.

Wendy laughed. "I knew they must hurt as much coming off as they do on," she told the helpless slave. "Enjoy it while you can, scum." Then she walked back to the front of the room and continued with a new lesson on proper grooming.

Two more hours passed before the evening's class was finally over. Wendy had the four slaves turn around to face the sling. It was a good lesson for them as well, she said to herself. She didn't expect to have any trouble from any of them again.

First, she roughly pulled the dildo out of Margot's ass. Margot was too exhausted to do anything but whimper. "You're lucky I'm feeling very nice tonight," Wendy told her. "Any other time I would have ordered you to clean it off with your tongue."

The handcuffs came off next. Margot's arms were so swollen and stiff she could not move them. Roughly Wendy pushed them down beside her body and, again, Margot could only whimper. When she was shoved out of the sling, her knees gave out and she feel to the floor. Wendy left her there and pulled off the mask.

Margot didn't even look human. Her hair was plastered to her head with sweat and her skin was a horrible mottled red. Her eyes were swollen and red-rimmed from crying. Her face was smeared with tears and mucous and there was blood on her chin from the cut on her tongue. Her lips were swollen and she moved her jaw painfully.

"I hope we've learned something here tonight," Wendy said.

"Yes, Mistress." It was a whisper through painful lips.

"Go clean yourself up," Wendy ordered. "You make me sick looking at you." She held out the horrible leather mask. "Clean this up as well, and hurry back."

"Yes, Mistress," Margot said, and immediately struggled to her feet and took the mask. Walking stiffly, she hurried out the door. They could hear water running down the hall and shortly afterward, Margot hurried back. Her face was washed but still mottled red, her lips and tongue swollen. Immediately she dropped to her knees before Wendy, put her head down, and offered the cleaned leather mask.

"Thank you, slave," Wendy said, taking it and hanging it back up on its peg on the wall.

"May I have permission to speak, Mistress?" Margot asked.

Wendy thrilled to hear her. "Yes, slave," she said.

"Mistress, I'm sorry." It was difficult for her to form the words with her tongue so badly swollen. "I'm sorry I acted the way I did. I have learned my lesson. I am a slave. You are my Mistress. I will not forget that."

Wendy didn't think she'd ever heard sweeter words. "Don't ever forget, slave," she said. "Now, class, you are dismissed."

She watched as they chimed, "Thank you, Mistress," then stood up to leave. It had been a very important night for all of them. Brenda, Alicia, and Ellen had learned an essential lesson about how ruthless their teacher could be if provoked. Leslie had discovered her true identity. And Margot, who had been such a worthless waste of time, had started to blossom into the truly magnificent slave that both Leah and Wendy had known she had the potential to become. Once again Wendy felt the leather catsuit grow warm and wet between her legs.

"All but you," Wendy indicated to Brenda as the slaves passed out the door in front of her.

"Thank you, Mistress," Brenda replied gratefully, and immediately knelt on the floor, ready for a command. With all her heart, she hoped that the spot before her mistress' door would be hers again this night.

Wendy watched as the slaves dressed, carefully fastening the top buttons of their shirts so that the leather collars would not be visible. She then stood at the top of the stairs as they filed out of the house into the cool, black night.

She turned and walked back to the classroom, taking off the skin-hugging catsuit as she went. Her nipples were hard and she tweaked them with her fingers, then went inside. Brenda, she knew, would be only too eager to take care of the rest.

"PURCHASES"
(from *Necessary Evil*)

Jennifer Dobson is a submissive who has found that her Mistress, while cruel, is also unimaginative and predictable. Jennifer meets Lyla Kirk and decides that Lyla's aggressive character could possibly be nurtured into that of a full-fledged Mistress. Fortunately for Jennifer, she is correct, and slowly Lyla moves into her new-found role.

"You know," Mistress Lyla says, "one of the real joys of going on these trips is when you do get a little time to yourself, you can do some shopping."

It is late Wednesday afternoon, and we are in Toronto. That by itself would be new to me, for it is the first time I have done a trade show in this largest

Canadian city. What makes it even fresher for me is that once again, Cleo and I are accompanied by the accounting department's Lyla Kirk—my Mistress Lyla.

As always, Cleo and I were first into the convention center, making sure our booth was set up and everything ready to go for the customary just-after-dawn push that always put us ahead of the competition. Now that everything was in order, we had a few hours to relax.

This time our rooms were in one of the finest hotels in the city, and I wondered how much leverage Mistress Lyla had used when they were chosen. As soon as Cleo saw the huge bathtub with its whirlpool jets, she decided that a hot, bubbly bath was definitely more interesting than going shopping before dinner. We decided on a time and place to meet for our evening meal, and then at Mistress Lyla's demand, she and I set out to see the sights.

The downtown streets were crowded and for this reason, Mistress Lyla quietly gave me permission to address her without the respectful title. Just as respectfully, I thanked her. She had given me similar permission while we were in the airport, on the plane, and inside the convention center. Of course, during this trip her permission was just a formality, for we were "on the job" at this point and calling her Mistress would definitely have been the wrong thing to do in front of others at the show.

But that was not the point. Everything depended on the fact that Mistress Lyla gave me the command to dispense with the title. By doing this, I was still under her orders. Tomorrow, I know that she will give me such a command before we leave to work the grueling hours of the trade show. At times, when we are presenting our line of fasteners to prospective clients, it will sometimes appear that Cleo and I are her superiors within our company. But once we are back in the hotel and I go back to her room with her, the charade will be over.

Before we left the hotel we stopped by Cleo's room to invite her along, but she begged off, citing the whirlpool. "We will see you at dinner, then," my dominatrix said.

"Yes," Cleo replied, and then added, "Mistress," before she closed the door.

Mistress Lyla was puzzled as we walked down the hall together. "Why did she call me that?" she asked.

"Because you are a dominatrix, Mistress," I replied. Permission to dispense with the title was not given when we were alone in the hotel, when others could not hear us, and I was glad to use the term again.

"But I am not her superior," Mistress Lyla said. "She belongs to someone else, doesn't she?"

"She does, Mistress," I replied, as I pushed the button to summon the elevator. "But as submissives, we are inferior to all dominatrixes, whether they directly control us or not. It is a term of respect. From now on, whenever you meet a submissive and she knows that you are a dominatrix, she will address you as 'Mistress.' She risks both your wrath and the anger of her own superior if she does not."

"My wrath?"

"Mistress," I said, "dominatrixes don't take another's slave without her permission, or abuse another's slave enough to cause serious injury, or give a command that counters one already given by the owner. At least, they usually don't. But if you met another dominatrix's slave and that slave was rude to you, what would you do?"

"Well," Mistress Lyla said, thinking about it, "I would probably get very angry."

"Wouldn't you be inclined to teach her a lesson? Perhaps a good slap across the face?"

"That would probably be my immediate reaction," my Mistress said.

"And," I continued, "there is not a dominatrix in the world who would not expect you to do that. Of course, once you had done that, you would probably be invited to help that dominatrix beat the shit out of the slave, just to make sure the lesson was learned."

Mistress Lyla said nothing more, for the elevator had arrived, but all the way down to the lobby I could see that the idea had definitely taken root.

And now we are out on the street, walking up the sidewalk and looking over this fascinating city. It has a "gay village" and before long it becomes obvious that we are in the center of it. When I see two women holding hands I am elated, and the more I look around, the more lesbians I see. My trained eyes don't take long to see the dominatrixes walking with their submissives a few respectful steps behind them, and I hope desperately that people will recognize us. I am so proud of my Mistress that I wish I was walking in chains, led by her with a leash.

There are stores here that sell leather goods and erotic books, and it puzzles me that my Mistress does not stop in them. Instead, I notice that she has a piece of paper in her hand and that she is looking intently at the street signs.

"Forgive me," I say—although I am sure I could use the term Mistress here, in this friendly place, I am under command not to use it and so I obey—"but are you looking for something specific?"

"I am," my Mistress says, and when she does not elaborate I ask no more, but follow her as she looks up and down the street. Finally she stops a police officer waiting on the corner and asks; she directs us down a side street and then up another street that is small enough to be just an alley.

"Are you sure this is correct?" I ask. It seems like we are lost, until my Mistress notices the small sign hanging over a doorway up ahead. It is this that she is searching for.

I breathe deeply as soon as we walk through the door into the store. It is the smell of hundreds of pieces of leather and it is intoxicating.

The weather here, while not as stifling as the summer heat back in our Southern home, is still in the low eighties, and the store is not air conditioned. The leather scent is almost overwhelming and I smile. It is a musk that I would happily drown in. It is the smell of both submission and domination at the same time.

There is a lovely woman at the cash register, dressed simply in a tank top and shorts; she assesses us instantly and immediately gives all of her attention to my Mistress. For me there is not even a glance, and I know that my status is obvious.

"Is there something I can help you with?" she asks.

"There certainly is," Mistress Lyla smiles. "I will be honest with you; I am new at this, and I own practically nothing. I have come here to rectify that."

The woman smiles, and I notice that it is the smile of solidarity. Submissives fight for the right to grovel at her feet, I am sure. "We have everything you will ever need," she says.

This is obvious. The store seems small, but I soon realize that there are rooms behind the one we are in. This first one is filled with shoes of every description. Most of them have shockingly high heels, all of them stiletto-thin. Their heels look razor-sharp and I long to see them on Mistress Lyla's feet, with those heels in my mouth, my Mistress ordering me to clean them, to fellate them.

In one small section near the bottom are shoes that fascinate me, for I have not seen anything like these before. Segregated from the powerful high-heeled shoes, they are obviously for slaves only. Black, ugly, heavy, there is a whole range of them and all of them look terribly uncomfortable. Several pairs of them have rings set into the leather, meant for hobbling. One of them, when I dare to peek into it, has hideous, sharp studs inside to tear into a submissive's feet once she stands in them. I shudder and hope that Mistress Lyla doesn't take a liking to these.

A little further into the room is a collection of harnesses, all of them tacked onto the wall with the prices beside them. Some are for the men who cower at the feet of dominant men or women: cockrings, ball harnesses, belts with studded pouches. Others are for women, and these intrigue me. There are leather bras with buckles to squeeze the tits into painful points. There are chastity belts that lock around a cunt. There are harnesses and blindfolds, wrist and ankle cuffs, and even a horrible leather hood with a zipper across the mouth. I shudder. I have seen all of these items before and have worn some of them, but seeing them all displayed on the wall at once gives me a delicious chill.

My Mistress is now in another room and I hurry to follow her. This room is mostly clothing for dominatrixes, and she is going through the racks as the clerk points out particularly interesting items. Their selection is stunning. I can see everything from suits that outfit from head to toe in leather, to costumes made up of only a few well-placed straps.

In the middle of everything is a large, square glass-fronted counter. The clerk and my Mistress are busy and ignoring me, so I move over to the counter for a look. It takes my breath away.

One side of the counter is dedicated to whips. They have every description here, lovingly laid out on a bed of white satin to show off the shining black leather. There are riding crops, bullwhips, small personal sticks, and in one corner, a majestic cat-o'-nine-tails, its cruel plumage streaming out over the white satin. There is even a whip with a tiny metal barb set into the end of it. That makes my blood run cold when I think of the damage it would do.

Another side is gags and blindfolds, ball gags of every size, goggles, eye covers and full-face masks in leather, cotton, and shiny rubber.

The third side is gloves: long leather gauntlets, satin gloves with eight buttons up the arms, fingerless leather gloves, gloves with studs over the knuckles. There is even a chain-mesh glove, such as the type that butchers wear, and I shudder to think about how it might be used.

The fourth side is an assortment of items. There are buttplugs in all sizes and dildos, by themselves or on leather harnesses. There are ben-wah balls, vibrators, condoms, lubricants. There are all sorts of rings to be worn in pierced nipples, labia and foreskins. And in one corner, all by itself, is a small item that at first I do not recognize. When I get closer I notice that it is a tiny branding iron. The sweat that breaks out on my forehead isn't from the heat.

"Jennifer!" The voice breaks me out of my daze and I hurry over to where my Mistress is waiting with the clerk. That young woman has a tape measure in her hands.

I am measured, completely. The thin dress I am wearing is no impediment and shortly the clerk is jotting down my bust size, my waist size, my height. "Now I'm sure there are other things you'd like to look at in the store," my Mistress says, and I take the not-so-subtle hint and walk back into the first room, where the shoes are. I catch another glimpse of those slave hobble boots and I am thankful that my shoe size was not included in the measurements.

When we leave, my Mistress hands me the large bag to carry. It is heavy and I long to peek inside, but I know better. I can only think about it as we find our way back to the crowded main street. I am thrilled to see that we are walking back to the hotel.

In the lobby, we only get quick glances from the staff and other guests as we walk in, but I feel as if all eyes are upon me. Surely they notice that I am a step behind her! And they have to know what kind of merchandise is in this bag! I can't believe that the whole world doesn't know that we are Mistress and slave, on our way upstairs together.

In the elevator we are alone. "Is the bag heavy?" she asks me.

"Oh, no, Mistress," I say to her.

"Fine," she says, but there is a coldness to her voice. I shudder, half in fear and half in elation. I am amazed at how quickly she is turning into a wickedly cunning dominatrix.

We reach the door to our suite. Only one room has been reserved for both of us. I still don't know what the sleeping arrangements will be, and I do not dare ask, but I do know that there is only one king-sized bed. I highly doubt that I will be asked to take it or even to share it.

Mistress Lyla opens the door and stands back. I step through it, but before I am even over the threshold, she pushes me so hard from behind that I fall to my knees on the carpet. The bag flies off and lands beside a chair.

"Mistress?" I cry out. My knees are on fire from sliding across the rug and my wrists hurt from the fall.

She closes the door quietly behind her. "That's exactly it," she says. "I'm supposed to punish you when you don't do what you're told—isn't that correct?"

"Yes, Mistress," I say to her.

"And you were told to call me Lyla, were you not?"

"Yes, Mistress, I was," I say.

"But in the elevator," she says, as she slips off her shoes, "you called me Mistress."

"I thought," I say, "that since we were alone, it would be respectful of me to use that term. I thought I had permission."

"You are correct; it would be respectful," she admits, "and from here on, you are to use it again, until we are in a situation where it would not be discreet. But even though it was respectful, you had not been given permission to use it. Permission is not an automatic thing, Jennifer."

I drop my eyes. "I am sorry, Mistress," I say. "Please forgive me."

"Well, there will be forgiveness, but I will have to punish you first," Mistress Lyla says. Then, just for a moment, the dominatrix is gone and she is just Lyla Kirk, still new to everything, still feeling the newfound power of her position. "That's right, isn't it?" she asks. "I'm supposed to think of things to punish you for, aren't I?"

"Mistress," I say, "this is everything I dreamed it would be."

She regains her haughty composure almost immediately. She amazes me every time I see her, and I know that I will see very few of these momentary lapses from now on.

"Then I think you will hand me that bag," she says. "No, wait. I think I would rather have it brought in your mouth, like a dog would fetch it."

I start toward the bag, but my Mistress adds, "Naked, please," and so I stop and slip off my clothes before I continue. The carpet, chosen to be long-wearing, is rough and burns my already sore knees.

The plastic bag has fallen so that the handles are flat on the floor and it is very difficult to pick it up between my teeth. For just a moment I consider lifting it with my hand, for my Mistress is behind me and she wouldn't be able to see it. But that would be contrary to my orders, and so I struggle to catch it between my teeth. When I finally lift it, it is heavy and the plastic slips out of my mouth. I have to bend down and go through the whole routine again, but this time I make sure that I have a firm hold on it.

"Good doggie!" my Mistress crows. Once again I am heartened by how quickly she falls into the role. I sit on my haunches before her, with the bag still in my mouth. She takes it from my hands.

"I bought some presents for you," she continues, as she opens the bag. "You know, I've always liked dogs. They're good companions and they can be a lot of fun. That's why I thought I might like to have one here with me, on this trip."

The first item that comes out is a leather collar. It is heavy, chrome-studded, with a large buckle and a ring for a leash. "Come here," she says.

I move forward, happily, on my hands and knees. When she drops her hand I know it to be a command that I am to sit, which I do. She reaches down and buckles the collar about my throat. It is very loose and hangs down on my chest.

"Mistress, may I speak freely?" I ask, hesitantly.

"You may," she says.

I take a deep breath. "If I may be so bold," I say, "I believe that you underestimate how much punishment I am capable of taking. We have a prearranged signal, the one we discussed, which I am to show you if I can't tolerate the level we reach."

"I know that," she says.

"I have not given you the signal, Mistress," I say, bowing respectfully. "I am nowhere near that plateau."

"I understand," she says. I am happy. Prior to this, she might have dropped her composure and asked me what she should do. But this time, she accepts it all as taken, as a Mistress receiving a deferential comment from her slave.

She unbuckles the collar and tightens it around my throat. Now I can feel the leather against my skin and I feel complete within the its circle. I love it when a Mistress places a collar around my neck. When it is Mistress Lyla I am giddy with joy.

"Of course," she adds, "I will now have to punish you for suggesting that."

"Thank you, Mistress," I say. Punishment is exactly what I am looking forward to.

Next out of the bag is a leash. This is snapped on to the ring on my collar. "I suppose that since you haven't had a walk today, you'll need one," she says, and she starts to walk.

The room is very large and Mistress Lyla goes all around it. Her stride is long and it is difficult for me to keep up with her. At first she slows down when I start to drop behind, but soon she is tugging hard on the leash to make me hurry. It pulls on my neck and I struggle to move faster. At one point she almost drags me. I am joyous.

Then we stop, and she loops the leash around the arm of a chair. "Stay," she says, as she might to a dog. Then she picks up the bag and walks into the other room. I sit, obediently, wondering what is coming next. My pussy is sopping and throbbing so much that I can hardly stand it. I wish I had the nerve, while under a Mistress's command, to touch it and possibly relieve some of the pressure. But I am too well trained and my hand won't move even close to that swollen, sex-starved nubbin.

She takes so long that I can hardly stand to wait. But wait I do, and I will wait all night if that is how long it takes her to come out. I have not been given permission to rise.

When she finally comes out I bow down on the carpet before her, whispering, "Mistress!" It is an automatic reaction when I see the goddess that stands before me.

She has purchased the outfit I caught a glimpse of

on the way out. It is made up completely of thin leather straps, joined with heavy chromed rings and decorated with thin chrome chains. One strap goes around her chest, attached to straps that go on either side of her delicious breasts to form an open bra. Straps weave down her belly and slip between her legs to cover that wonderful pussy. The chains circle her waist and attach to the straps at her back. On her feet she has a pair of impossibly high, stiletto-heeled shoes in shiny black patent leather. On her hands are fingerless gloves, the ones with chrome studs across the knuckles. She wears a black leather cap and her dark hair flows luxuriously out from under it.

"You like my outfit, yes?" she says, as she stands and models it. I have never seen anything so stunning in my life and I am sure my eyes are still huge. I can't get enough of the sight of her in it. My pussy aches and my mouth waters at the sight of her cunt, covered by that strip of thin black leather. I long to lick those shoes and have those stiletto heels push hard against my tongue.

She walks over and stands right by me, so close that I can see the moisture on her cunt hairs and smell the rich perfume. "You want that, don't you?" she says.

"Yes, Mistress," I whisper. She brings herself so close that my tongue, stretched out to reach her, just misses the hot folds. Then she spins about and walks away. I sigh heavily, until I realize that she has picked up another purchase, a heavy black leather paddle.

"Spanking is nice," she says, "but I just couldn't resist this." She slaps it gently against her hand, but even that light blow results in a hefty smacking sound. I can almost feel it against my asscheeks. I want it so badly, so badly, and she walks toward me with it in her hand...

...and then, just as quickly, she looks at her watch and puts the paddle down. "We're going to be late for dinner," she says, and abruptly she walks back into the other room.

I feel tears in my eyes. She was just steps away with that paddle, and now I have to wait. When she comes back she is fully dressed, but at the last moment she opens a button on her shirt. The leather harness is under it and I sigh with longing.

Now she unbuckles the collar and orders me to stand up. My throat feels naked without it. She leaves the collar on the table, but she takes the leash and ties it tightly around my waist. "Now dress," she says, and I slip on my clothes over the leather restraint.

I can feel it, as hot as wanting, as we walk down the hallway. Cleo is already in the dining room when we arrive, and she respectfully stands when Mistress Lyla comes into the room. She only sits down when my Mistress nods slightly to her, and it is obvious that my Mistress appreciates this treatment. It seems that she molds more into her role minute by minute.

Mistress Lyla puts her bag on the floor between my chair and hers. At one point, when I am reaching for my cocktail, I happen to glance down and go first cold and then searing hot right through. The handle of the paddle is sticking out of the top of it. Throughout the whole meal I sneak quick peeks at it, and Mistress Lyla notices and smiles.

Dinner takes forever, and the discussions about the trade show and how we are going to approach the customers tomorrow seem so far away for me. What do I care about clients, when my Mistress Lyla sits beside me wearing leathers and chains? How can I concentrate when I can feel the leather leash that she has wrapped around my waist? Who cares about product lines when there is a paddle beside me, a paddle that I know will be used later to tan my ass?

Once again Mistress Lyla makes me sit in a restaurant, almost overcome with longing, while she takes her time. The conversation flows only because she continues to talk about work and our role at the trade show. Cleo and I are professional about what we do, and in the past we have been able to talk easily about it even through cocktail parties, boring clients, and all-night emergency meetings. I am thankful now for that. I feel like someone else is talking and only when I listen to myself do I realize it is me. My whole being concentrates on my pussy.

Finally Mistress Lyla says, "It's getting late and we have an early start. If you will excuse me, Cleo, I would like to return to my room."

"Not at all," Cleo replies, and I hear the unspoken "Mistress" at the end of it. "It's time for me to turn in as well." She is grateful, for I know she is tired and there is no way she would ever suggest calling an end to the evening when a Mistress present in the room had not already done so. Such is the training we receive!

The elevator ride seems impossibly long and while we are in the small cubicle Cleo keeps silent, her eyes on the floor. When we stop, she turns to go to her room.

"Good night, Cleo," my Mistress says. Cleo looks around for a moment and sees that no one else is in the hallway. "Good night," she says, and then adds quietly, "Mistress."

I can't help but notice Mistress Lyla's smile at the word. I feel sorry for Cleo as she walks down the hallway to her room, by herself. I know that she has at least one video in her suitcase and there is a player in her room. But that is just a tape, and I have a real live Mistress here with me, taking me back to her room.

Mistress Lyla opens the door to the room. I follow her inside and stand, unsure, with no commands to follow.

"Undress," Mistress Lyla says, disappearing into the other room. When she comes back, her no-nonsense suit and her sensible shoes are gone. She is once again clad only in the spider's-web weaving of leather and chains, those shiny black leather shoes on her feet.

I have left the leash around my waist. Mistress Lyla grabs the end of it and uses it to pull me forcefully to the floor. She buckles the collar back around my throat, then unwraps the leash and puts it back in its rightful place. She uses this to walk me, like a dog, into the bedroom.

The bed is huge and inviting, but I am not asked to get on to it. Instead, she ties the leash to a chair so that I can get close to the bed but can't quite touch it.

"On the chair," she says, and pushes me—not quite a kick—with the toe of one shoe when I don't understand what she means. Finally I understand and hurry to obey. I am now lying across the chair with my ass in the air. It is the same position I took when she spanked me.

This time there is not the mercy of a bare hand. Instead, I close my eyes and wait, for I know what is coming. When it does, it sucks the breath right out of me.

Wham! The paddle comes down hard on my skin and I cry out. It really hurts. She smacks again, twice more, once on each cheek, then stands back to examine her work.

"Very nice," she says appraisingly. "That clerk was

right, this is much better than just a spanking." She touches my burning buttocks with her hand; her touch is cool and comforting on my skin. "You should see this, Jennifer. It's all a nice mottled red. Well, I think I can do better than that."

She does. The paddle cracks down over and over on my battered flesh. Tears course down my cheeks and I sob. Finally I cry out, "Mercy, please, Mistress!"

"Is that a signal for clemency?" she asks, the paddle raised to strike again.

"No, Mistress!" I sob. "It is a plea from your slave for mercy!"

"Then it is of no interest to me," she says, and brings the paddle down hard. My ass is on fire, and my pussy is as well. She knows this and she rubs the handle of the paddle against my slit. I moan as the hot chills go through me, and almost involuntarily I push my cunt hard against it. She pulls the paddle away. "This is for my pleasure, not yours," she says. She grabs my collar and pulls me to the floor. I cry out when my pummeled cheeks hit the carpet. It is as if I am sitting on live coals.

"This," she continues, "is for my pleasure also." She makes sure I am watching as she reaches into her bag and brings out a large, battery-powered vibrator.

"The paddling," she says, "is because you called me Mistress when you were told not to. I also told you that I would have to punish you for suggesting that I tighten the collar. That is what this is for."

I am confused; the vibrator is something I use for pleasure, not punishment. But her reasoning is immediately apparent when she pushes the leather strap away from her wet pussy and turns the dial that makes the vibrator buzz.

"I know how much you enjoy licking me," she says, as she sits down on the edge of the bed facing me. The vibrator buzzes up against her swollen, delightful lips. "I know that you like to put your tongue on me and taste my juice. I know that you like to suck my clit and push your tongue into my hole. You do, don't you?"

"Yes, Mistress," I whisper. My tongue is licking my lips now, wishing it were those other hairy lips that my eyes are glued to.

"It would give you such gratification to be able to pleasure me," she continues. The vibrator has pushed apart her pussylips and I can see the sweet pink edge of her clit. I can all but taste its salty heat in my mouth. "You want this cunt. You want to taste it, lick it, fuck it. But you can't. I'm going to get my pleasure from this vibrator, and you can only sit there and watch."

This is a cruel and cunning punishment indeed. I would give anything to be there between her legs. When she trembles, I want to be sending those chills up her spine. I want to suck on her nipples and work my way down to her hairy recess. Instead, I am tied to the chair, my ass blistered, forced to watch as my Mistress casts me aside in favor of an electrical device.

She is as noisy and as exuberant as always and when she comes I moan aloud, but this time in agony instead of ecstasy. She makes me kiss the vibrator and I savor it, licking her thick, wine-rich juices off the warm plastic surface.

"It's time for bed," she says, as she slips the leather straps off in preparation. "That wake-up call comes very early." She will sleep naked, obviously in the bed, and I wonder where I will be permitted to sleep.

It doesn't take long to find out. She takes the leash and makes me crawl to the foot of the bed, where she ties the leash around the post. I will sleep on the floor, but as long as I am alongside my sleeping Mistress I am happy.

I am afraid, however, that I underestimate the latent cruelty I have helped to awaken. She has one more trick in her bag, one that is so original it takes my breath away.

"You recognize these, of course," she says, as she stands over me, holding them.

Of course I do. They are tie-wraps, thin plastic straps with a loop at one end. They are used to neatly tie electrical wires together; once the loose end is inserted into the loop, they can be tightened to any circumference. The loop is one-way; the wrap can always be tightened further, but it will not loosen. Our company sells them and they are our number-one product. They are the main reason why Cleo and I attend trade show after trade show, selling clients on their quality.

Up until now I had never thought of them as having any uses other than the industrial ones. But now, as Mistress Lyla makes me lie on my side on the carpet, the familiar little devices are as nasty and heartless as any item I have seen in SM catalogues.

She puts one around each ankle, not so tight that it would leave marks, but enough that I can feel it. Then one goes around each wrist, and I am ordered to curl into a ball. Now she takes one more, and uses it to bind all four together.

My arms and wrists are joined as one, and I cannot move. I long to stretch out my legs, but they will not move. My spine is curved, doubled over, and my arms are out straight. The position is uncomfortable right from the start, but Mistress Lyla has put me in it, and I will suffer it uncomplaining all night. I love her so much!

I can't look up, and I imagine how she looks, so beautiful in her nakedness as she stands before the mirror and brushes out her long hair. I hear the sheets rustle as she gets into bed. "Jennifer," she says, "you can't imagine how soft this bed is! And the pillows are so comfortable. I'm going to sleep like a baby."

Then the lights go out, and I can hear her breathing become deep and regular as she goes to sleep. My arms are numb and my legs ache. My bruised buttocks throb uncontrollably and my poor pussy is about to burst with unrelieved pressure. My throat is encircled with a leather collar and I am lying on my side on the floor. I have never been happier in my life.

"BARCELONA, SPAIN"
(from *A Victorian Romance*)

A Victorian Romance tells the story of Elaine, a young woman who is treated to a trip abroad by her lesbian aunt. As the pair stay with the aunt's friends, young acquaintances introduce Elaine to special pleasures. Elaine recounts these in letters to her best friend.

Barcelona, Spain

Dearest Alicia,

Does my handwriting look even better today, does my attitude seem even cheerier and more excited? It must, Alicia, for I am so thrilled to be here, in this lovely city, and I am sure that I shall not see a prettier one ever again, no matter how far I travel.

Our ship arrived in the harbor yesterday; and it was so exciting to be met by smaller ships, all of them with flags waving in a nautical greeting, and to be guided by them into the port. All of the people on our ship lined the deck, Auntie and myself included, and we spent much time waving to the crews on these vessels, and enjoying the sunshine and the panorama of the city afforded us from the water.

It is always wonderful when history, which is so dry and boring when fed to us by our teachers from the dusty volumes at school, is actually before one; and this was the case with me, for this is the port from which Christopher Columbus left when he traveled forth and discovered the New World; and to that end, there is a huge monument to him, of a tall column with his image atop, erected just two years ago; and it is thrilling to look about myself and realized that this is the very place he left from, although it definitely would have looked much different those four hundred years ago, for it is now a bustling city, and much modernized today.

As always, Auntie had made arrangements well in advance of our arrival, and a carriage was waiting, with footmen to attend to our trunks. This time it was sent by Auntie's good friend Señorita Navarro, who was waiting at her home for us to arrive.

The large estates here are called "villas," and Señorita Navarro's home certainly qualified for that title. It was closer to the outskirts of the city, and the carriage ride was quite a long but fascinating one, affording me endless views of this beautiful city. Here the women seem to prefer brighter clothes, and the buildings are painted mostly in cheerful pastel colors, so that it is as different from our somber London streets and gray-coated British women as you can possibly imagine; the climate is much warmer, all of the year, than it is at home, and this seems to give the people a more jaunty spirit and this, combined with their quick Spanish tongue, made me feel as if I were in the center of an exciting foreign play.

But I digress, for we arrived at the villa, and what a sight it was. It lay at the bottom of a small hill, nestled into bright green fields, surrounded by exquisite wrought iron fences; and the house itself was neither brick nor stone, but covered with a thick plaster that had been painted a muted shade of pink, with a red-tiled roof and brilliant white accents.

As I have mentioned, the Spanish are very outgoing and friendly; and I have been used to arriving at the doors of Auntie Lydia's friends, and being greeted by the servants and walking indoors into the parlor to meet the mistress of the household; but this is Barcelona, and everything is different here. As soon as she heard the sound of the carriage coming up to the villa, Señorita Navarro flung the door open herself, and rushed outside to greet us; and Auntie Lydia had barely found her footing upon the ground when she was swept up into her friend's ample bosom, with many hugs and kisses being exchanged between the two. Then it was my turn, and I as well was crushed in the woman's firm grip, and kissed and welcomed with a mixture of accented English and delightful Spanish.

We retired inside of the villa, which was as sumptuous inside as out, and were given small glasses of sweet Spanish sherry to sip, while Aunt Lydia recounted our adventures so far to our hostess (who, every now and again, put down her glass and came over to hug my Auntie again).

Señorita Navarro had a surprise of her own, and I could not help but smile at her own broad, infectious grin; for it turned out that she had arranged for a party to welcome us, and it would be held at one of the fanciest restaurants in the city. I was charmed by the suggestion, for the excitement of parties and all-night affairs was still very strong within me; and when I glanced over at Aunt Lydia I had to bite my tongue to prevent a giggle from escaping, for Aunt Lydia was trying her best to smile and assure her hostess that the party was a most welcome surprise; for on the carriage-ride over, Aunt Lydia had told me in confidence that traveling, while very exciting, can also be tiring, and she was looking forward to a quiet evening in Señorita Navarro's home, and an early night to bed. But Auntie is as well-versed in the rules of etiquette as any socialite, and Señorita Navarro was convinced that my Auntie looked forward to the party as eagerly as a hungry cat looks at a sardine.

Aunt Lydia did manage to request a nap to refresh her from the journey, however, and I later discovered that afternoon rests are quite common in this country; and so following a light luncheon we were shown to our rooms. Mine was a lovely blue one, with a heavy, dark-wooded bed, and airy linen upon it; and although I did not believe that I would be able to sleep, my eyes closed soon after my head touched the pillow—and soon after, my special friend assisted me to relieve the mounting pressure in my cunny.

When I awoke, the shadows had lengthened considerably, and when I dressed and made my way to the parlor, I found the house empty save for a maid, who informed me that my hostess and my Auntie were outside. Indeed they were, walking through the

large and well-tended gardens at the back of the villa;
and I started down to greet them, until I noticed
them together; for they were walking with their arms
about each other, their conversation punctuated occasionally with tiny kisses; they would stop every now
and again to examine a particularly beautiful flower, or
a well-trimmed shrub; and I stayed back, not wanting
to disturb them; and instead, I watched them from a
distance, and longed for the day that I would be able
to visit the friends I had made on this journey again,
for a second and third and perhaps, as Aunt Lydia
had, uncountable times, to hold them close to me and
kiss them gently, and be so familiar and content in
their presence that simply wandering throughout the
garden and looking at the flowers with them would be
a sensuous experience.

Eventually they returned to the house, and we
dressed for the party. It was to be very formal, and I
wore the exquisite dress presented to me when I went
to the Opera in Paris, while Auntie wore an equally
lovely dress I had not seen before; and Señorita
Navarro dressed in the formal fashion of her country,
which was a very bright, multicolored outfit with long
skirts and an elegantly embroidered bolero jacket.
Again we took the long carriage-ride back into the
city, which was now alight and alive with people,
refreshed from their siestas (which I discovered was
the Spanish name for the afternoon rest) and ready to
enjoy the evening.

As I mentioned before, the party was held at a very
fancy and expensive restaurant, and all of the guests
were women, as was to be expected; and while the
number of guests was enormous, and the crowd
seemed to be expanding all the time as carriages

pulled up to the entrance, it also seemed that Aunt Lydia knew all of them, and I was introduced to so many women that after a while it all became a blur; and between the glass of strong wine I was given, and the sound of so many voices, some speaking English, some Spanish, and the warmth of the room, I soon became quite giddy, and chose a quiet corner in which to sit and regain my bearings.

I sat for a moment, and composed myself; and then I was aware of a hand upon my shoulder; and a sweet, lightly accented voice said, "Are you all right? Is there anything I can do?"

I looked up, Alicia, and found a young woman standing over me, her beautiful face filled with concern for me. "Oh, I think that the room was a bit too warm for me," I said. "I am feeling much better now, thank you; I simply needed to sit down."

My benefactress pulled up a chair and sat beside me. "I know what you mean," she said. "Gatherings of this type can be exciting, but they can also be over-whelming. And very hot." I adored my fancy silk party gown, but at that moment I was very envious of her fine native costume, which was as elaborate as mine, but much looser and comfortable.

"I am very sorry," I said, "I am afraid that my condition has affected my manners also. I am Elaine Dickey, and I am here with my aunt, Lydia Knight."

"So you are Elaine!" she said, and she introduced herself as Renata. "Yes, I know your aunt very well, and I was told that she was bringing her niece along on this trip. I am very pleased to meet you."

We chatted for some time, and Alicia, I must admit that I was very pleased that she was there; for she was the only person at the party close to my age, all of the other guests being of my Auntie's generation; and while they were certainly a long way from being elderly, she is after all my Mother's sister, and I know from experience that I would much rather be entertained by my own friends than by the friends of my parents. Renata knew this as well, and commented upon it. When I agreed with her, she said, "I have been invited to a party not far from here, and all of the guests are closer to our age; would you like to accompany me to it?"

I looked around at the crowded room, at my Auntie conversing gaily with her own friends, and I found the idea most intriguing. "But I shall have to ask my Auntie first, for she is my guardian," I said, and Renata agreed to go with me to beg her permission.

Under any other circumstances, she would not have allowed me to go off without her on my first day in a new city, Aunt Lydia said; but since I would be with Renata—a young woman whom Auntie greeted with a hug, and obviously trusted—I was more than welcome to attend. However, the permission came about only after I saw Auntie give Renata a look which I did not comprehend at all; and when Renata nodded, Auntie stepped back and thought about something for a little while; and only when she had obviously come to a decision in her own mind did she say yes. Renata also asked when Auntie would be returning to Señorita Navarro's villa; and when Auntie said that she was not sure, Renata assured her that she would take me to the villa in her own carriage, which was acceptable to Auntie. And once all of that was done, Alicia, I bid good-bye to the hostess of the party (a very lovely lady named Señorita Marquez) and gratefully exited the building into the cooler air of the evening.

Renata called up her carriage, and soon we were traveling through the beautiful old city, which my companion told me is currently undergoing an almost complete revival; and indeed, it was easy to see that many of the buildings had recently been restored to the condition they had been in when built so many years ago, while many others were in the process of undergoing such work. There was so much happening on the streets that I could not believe it; people entering homes, restaurants, gathering in groups on the street corners to speak with each other, or young lovers simply out strolling, hand in hand, to enjoy the pleasure of the clear summer evening.

Our carriage stopped before a private villa, a huge one that was just as lovely as Señorita Navarro's; and Renata explained to me that it belonged to a young socialite in the city, who held parties of this type on a regular basis, and which were very popular among ladies of the city. I asked what type of party she could be referring to, for I was firmly of the belief that a party is always just a gathering of people who did so to enjoy themselves, and could not comprehend any other type.

At this, Renata became quite serious, and held my hand as she looked into my eyes and spoke to me. "Elaine, I am sure that you have never attended this type of party before, else you would not have asked me that. I do know that you share our secret, and you seem to be very open to any type of experience, which is why I have asked you here. However, I also understand that it may be too unusual for you; and should you feel that way, you must not be embarrassed to call me aside and tell me so; and if you do, I shall never think any less of you, but I will simply inform our hostess that you have forgotten something at Señorita Marquez's function—your purse, perhaps—and I will make our apologies and we shall leave, with no fear of mortification. Will you do that for me?"

"Of course," I said, confused at her cryptic message, and wondered at what type of diversion waited inside the innocent-looking villa; but as I have said before, Alicia, my secret has ignited a flame inside of me, and nothing is too bizarre that I will not, at the very least, entertain the thought!

We walked to the door of the house, and Renata rapped with the lion's-head knocker; the large, heavy door was opened by a young woman, obviously a servant, who greeted Renata and stepped aside so that we might enter. "I shall fetch my Mistress," she said, and we were left alone in the room, although not for long, for a woman close to my age, and clad only in a loose, brightly colored robe, came forth and hugged Renata heartily.

Her name was Juanita, and when I was introduced to her, she shook my hand, and then hugged her to me. "Welcome to my home, and welcome to my party," she said; but this was unusual to me, for there were no sounds of a gathering, and there had been no carriages outside, as had been at the restaurant where Señorita Marquez had held her court. "Have you ever been to such an event before?"

I was about to question this, but before I could, Renata broke in and replied in the negative. Juanita brightened up considerably at this, even though I did not comprehend her question in the least. "Then," she said, "we shall not lose any time, for the night is young, and so are we."

The maid took my wrap, and we made our way through the halls of the huge villa. It was only after we had gone a short distance that I was able to discern the sound of other people within the house; but at the same time, it did not seem to be normal conversation, but rather, a comforting sound of people enjoying themselves, and I thought that it might be a dinner party, with everyone making sounds of pleasure in their throats as they tasted the food; but as I was to find out very quickly, they were indeed sounds of pleasure, but it was not food that was being eaten.

We turned the corner, and found ourselves in a large room, with many smaller ones branching off it; and the gaslights had been set low, so that at first it was difficult to see; but as my eyes adjusted to the darkness, it was evident that the room contained a number of young women, and all of them enjoying themselves with each other!

There were several chairs, and chaise lounges, and even cushions upon the floor, and all were being used by women. On one lounge a woman lay, while another knelt upon the floor, her mouth firmly upon the prone woman's crotch. On another lounge were three women, all applying themselves to each other. Two women on the floor had a rubber friend which they were using to tease each other, while a woman sate upon a cushion, her head thrown back in delight as another fondled and sucked upon her nipples.

Did I shy away, Alicia? I may tell you now that I most certainly did not; and when Renata came up to me and whispered in my ear that I would not shame myself by requesting to leave should I not approve of the goings-on, I whispered back to her that only if the villa were on fire would I leave this room. She smiled, and then she put her arm around me, and kissed me soundly.

This kiss deepened swiftly, and I felt her tongue in my mouth, and my own rose to meet it, for I was so excited that I could not believe it; and who would not be, in a room filled with women enjoying sex, with the sound of their moans and gasps so loud, with the hot smell of their nectar rich and thick in the air? Then I felt another's hands upon me, and found that it was Juanita, and I kissed her too just as soundly, as Renata loosened the buttons of my fancy gown.

I was undressed almost before I knew it, and together, Renata and Juanita led me over to a lounge, where I was gently set down upon it, and given the opportunity to watch these women as they undressed each other. The whole room was alive with the wonder of sex, and two women who were walking past me stopped and fondled my breasts, one on either side of me; and occasionally they stopped and kissed each other passionately over top of me, then went back to sucking on my nipples; and I realized how very exciting this group sex was when they both kissed me hard and then got up and walked into one of the adjoining rooms—for it seems that there are no limits here, no boundaries, just everyone joined for the sole purpose of sexual enjoyment.

Very shortly Renata and Juanita were devoid of their clothing as well, and I admired their gorgeous bodies; for the Spanish have a bronze skin and beautiful dark hair, and these women were long-limbed and flat-bellied, and their breasts were firm, their nipples not pink like my own, but a lovely chocolate color, and I longed to have them in my mouth, and said so;

whereupon Juanita came close to me, and leaned over me, and allowed her bosom near my mouth; and I closed my eyes and sucked those hard tips into my lips; and while I did so, Renata spent the longest time just running her fingers over my body, and tarrying between my legs before commencing her caresses all over again.

"Let me taste you!" I begged, and Juanita was only too happy to oblige; and so within moments, she was kneeling upon the lounge, with her puss over my mouth, and I lost no time whatsoever in putting the tip of my tongue between those sweet fleshy folds and tickling that most intimate of all places with it. She obviously enjoyed my work, for she moaned quite loudly, and moved about, so that I was blessed with the moist folds of her cunny all over my face.

Renata was pressing her fingers inside of me, and pressing the hot center of my pleasure with her thumb; and the chills that went through me were delightful. I concentrated upon them, and upon Juanita's delicious nectar that now threatened to overflow my mouth; and so I could not tell just when the third woman came over to my side; but suddenly I was aware that a warm mouth was on my nipple, and a warm hand was fondling my bosom with a passion that matched my own superbly.

I could not see this woman who was affording me such pleasure, for Juanita was over top of me; and so I simply enjoyed her touch, and was even more excited at the realization that I was being fondled intimately by someone I not only did not know, but could not even see. Did you ever think that I would write such a line, Alicia? But it was true, true, and it only served to heighten my rapture.

I now reached up with my hands and held Juanita's smooth buttocks, and pulled her closer to me so that I might jam my tongue inside of her tunnel. I fucked her with my tongue, bouncing her bottom with my hands and relishing the heat and perfume even as my tongue was wet with her juice. She could not contain herself, and when she reached her climax, she cried out in Spanish and ground her mound upon me until I was completely lost in the rising fever of her spending.

She took a moment to catch her breath, and somewhat shaky in the wake of her explosion, she got up from the lounge. I was then able to see the woman who was so intent upon my bosom, and I could hardly believe it, and had to sit up and look at her again in my wonder.

Alicia, she was a Moor, and the first person of her race I had ever seen outside of the pictures in my schoolbooks. Her skin was dark, so black that it almost appeared shiny, and her hair was thick and black and wiry, not only the hair upon her head but upon her mound as well. Her name was Tania, she told me, in an accent that was at once both feverishly exotic, and also as cultivated and clipped as my own English one. By this time Renata had left my cunny and, kneeling behind Tania, she reached around her to caress her pert, firm breasts; and the contrast of skin colors amazed me, for I had never seen anyone like her.

She straddled me upon the couch, kneeling carefully over my chest and put on a delightful show of stroking her own nipples, pulling them out between her fingers and twisting them; and they were huge, Alicia, the largest I had ever seen, and I longed to suck upon them. She bent forward and rubbed them against my own, and my cunny throbbed with desire for her. Then she sat up straight again and used her fingers to pull apart the thick lips of her slit; and I was transfixed by the sight, for while my own puss was pink, hers was a vibrant rosy red, more like a cherry than anything, and deliciously ringed by her dark skin; and it gleamed wet with her juices. When she arranged herself over me and rubbed that rich red flesh over my nipples, my breasts were wet with her; and so I bent forward and licked her honey from my nipples, and savored the sweet taste in my mouth, and she came forward and kissed me with a ferocious wanting that matched my own.

At this moment, two women came up to Renata, one on either side of her, and began to kiss and caress her; and in the manner that was prevalent at this particular event, she left me alone with Tania and went with the two women into one of the adjoining rooms. With my new friend to myself, I allowed myself to sink deep into her kisses, and returned them lovingly as her tongue strained to touch against mine.

I felt delightfully wicked as I left the couch, and bade her to lie down upon it; and then I spent a tremendous amount of time just exploring her body, which was so foreign and fascinating to me. I marveled at the lighter skin of her palms and her feet, and sucked her fingers into my mouth one by one. I ran my tongue up and down her legs, stopping for a moment to taste the sweet nectar between her thighs, and teased her before returning to her legs. I kissed her belly and ran my hands over her arms, and spent a great deal of time at her breasts, for I was fascinated by her huge nipples, and pressed them together in the hopes of getting both of them into my mouth at once. When I did so, it was exquisite. They filled my mouth and my tongue could not move fast enough upon them.

I thought at first her skin would taste like chocolate; of course it did not, but it still seemed, so rich to my tongue that I could not get enough of her, and once I had covered her body once I had to start all over again. By now, though, she was asking to reciprocate, and suggested that I place myself over top of her, which I did with very little pleading on her part, for my cunny was so wanting and juicy that I could feel its heat and wetness and the throbbing went through my entire body.

She placed her tongue inside of my fleshy lips—a tongue that was so pink against her skin that it thrilled me—and I used my fingers to spread hers apart, as she had done earlier; and I spent so much time just marveling at the intensity and beauty of her cherry-red slit that she finally moved her hips to signal her need. I rubbed my fingers over her, at first gently, then with the force that she wanted, and pressed a digit into that velvety-smooth, hot, wet tunnel before applying my own mouth; and the taste of her was exotic and familiar at the same time, and so thrilling that you cannot imagine, Alicia!

"Eat me, Elaine! Oh, eat my cunny, please!" she gasped, taking out just a moment from my own intimate place, which she was giving most impressive attention with her tongue. Her words spurred me on, and I lost myself in the heat of her body, until I was aware that someone else was speaking to us.

I looked up, and saw a gorgeous Spanish woman, who was playing with her nipples and watching us intently. "Please," she said, in heavily accented, broken English, "please, I need."

"Of course," Tania said. "Elaine, would you object?" I did not know what she meant, but I had learned to say yes to anything, and did so right away. At Tania's request, I got up—slightly regretful, for I had been enjoying her tongue on my mound immensely —and lay down on the softly carpeted floor as Tania indicated.

Elaine, there are so many ways to make love, and I learned so many that night. Tania lay down on the floor with me, her mouth at my cunny so that she could continue giving me the pleasure I had so enjoyed before. The Spanish woman had her mouth at Tania's rosy red flesh, and I now had the pleasure of tasting yet another woman, for the Spanish woman positioned herself so that I might take her. We lay in this triangle on the floor, and it was certainly the best situation I had seen, for no one was left out; every mouth had a cunny to suck, and every cunny had a delightfully experienced tongue to provide the pleasure that was the intent of all.

Alicia, it was exciting enough to be in this love triangle with my new lovers; but remember that the whole room was filled with women in various positions with each other, and the air was loud with moans of delight, and with women laughing and begging for a tongue here, a hand here; and there was the delicious smell of feminine nectar. All of this added immensely to my gratification. One always wonders, with a new lover, if she measures up favorably to lovers in the past; and it was obvious, by my Spanish beauty's writhing and moaning, that my tongue was working her over in a manner that pleased her; and when she took a moment to whisper, "Oh, yes, yes, harder, my little one!" my whole body shivered.

Tania's tongue was still firmly upon mine, and every now and again she would use her fingers to rub and excite me, and then lick me again; and the alternating methods thrilled me to the core and built up the delicious pressure that I knew only a climax would relieve. As for my pleasure-giver, she was enjoying her own sensations courtesy of the Spanish tongue very firmly between her thighs, on that wet red cunny which I had so happily lapped at myself.

It was the Spaniard who spent first, and she moved about so much, and cried so loudly, that it was difficult for me to stay with her; but I did, and continued to lick at the pleasure button in her cunny until I had drawn every last shudder out of her lovely body. "Now it is your turn," she said, and moved aside, and Tania and I drew together, until once again I had my lips on her ruby warmth, and she on mine.

She was thoroughly soaked, and I had to fill my mouth with her delicious juices and taste her completely before I got down to the wonderful business of giving her pleasure. Her luscious button was huge, so large that I could suck it in between my lips, and gently nibble at it with my teeth, and hold it while I lashed its tip with my tongue. This resulted in squeals of delight, and an even more enthusiastic motion across my own button.

How much of this could I stand? By now my cunny was the very center of my body, and every nerve, every feeling began and ended there. By this time, Juanita was over us again, with a hand on each of us, fondling our breasts, tweaking our nipples, running her hand over ivory and ebony buttocks; and I could contain myself no longer, and spent with a fury, my tongue still in that ruby richness until Tania joined me in our climax.

I was as weak as if I had run a ten-mile race, and I actually sobbed with joy as first Juanita and then Tania took me into their arms and hugged and kissed me. It was obvious to the group that I was a newcomer, and several of the women came up to me and hugged me and welcomed me.

Very quickly I realized that they were not leaving again, and as I lay upon the thick carpet, I felt hands upon my body. Looking up, I saw that several women were around me, running their fingers over my skin. I started to sit up, but Juanita pressed me back gently, and kissed me. "We have a special greeting for those who come to us," she said softly. "Please, little one, lie back and enjoy."

What else was I to do, Alicia, but exactly as she said? With all of those soft hands upon me, I would not have moved for anything. There were hands upon my shoulders, fondling my bosom, mouths sucking on my nipples, working their way down to my wet mound, and when I felt soft lips upon my own I found they belonged to Renata. "Are you enjoying yourself, my friend?" she asked, and I could hardly find the words to tell her how happy I was that I had been invited into her secret world, to join this most fantastic party. But she placed a finger across my lips, and then replaced it with her mouth, and I submerged deep into the bliss and let everyone take me over.

Further and further I sank, and it seemed like a dream with all of those hands and lips and mouths on me, and I almost thought that if I opened my eyes, I

would see my own body as if I were outside of it.
There was a hot mouth on my cunny; and then firm
hands lifted my buttocks, and while one tongue
played upon my button, another probed the tight
pucker of my bottom. When I reached my climax for a
second time, it was almost unreal, and the women
marveled at my shivers and moans of delight.

We stayed at the party until well past midnight, but
it was hardly over; for Juanita invited any interested
persons to dress and join her, and when I asked the
reason, Renata suggested that I do so also, for it
would be the perfect introduction to Barcelona. I did,
and Juanita called for two coaches, for almost a dozen
of the guests were to leave with her, while almost that
many stayed behind to pursue their endeavors that
evening.

Our group was a varied one indeed; three or four
wore dresses as magnificent as my own, many more
wore their bright Spanish costumes, and two wore the
well-tailored suits which had become my clothing of
choice. Tania was dressed in a brilliantly colored loose
robe, which she told me was common in her own
country; and then we went out.

Our destination was a street in the center of town,
which seemed to have more people on it at this early
hour than our London streets do at noon. All were
obviously enjoying themselves, and most of the estab-
lishments on the street were lounges and restaurants,
with their doors and windows flung wide open to the
traffic on the streets. The night was hot, and when we
went inside the first restaurant it was very full, and
very noisy, with a band playing Spanish music upon
their guitars; and someone handed me a cool mug of
very rich beer, which went down as smooth as silk,

while another offered me tidbits on small plates, all manner of marinated vegetables and cooked fishes and meats, all somewhat salty, so that a second glass of beer was most appreciated.

I soon discovered that the idea was not to plop oneself in a single establishment and spend the evening drinking, as is the custom in our English pubs; instead, one took refreshment at one restaurant, and then once it was finished, went back out to the street to seek out the next. In this manner we had soon visited three or four places, and I was becoming quite giddy; and when we were at the fifth, I danced gaily with Tania and Renata and Juanita in turn, and could not imagine having more fun.

It was quite a shock to me, then, when we left yet another restaurant, that the sky was lightening with the approaching dawn. "My Auntie will be sick with worry!" I told Renata. "I must get back immediately."

"You need not have concern," Renata said and offered me a delicious sticky biscuit. "Your Auntie knows exactly what is going on, and she knows that I will allow no harm to come to you; for indeed, your Auntie has done exactly this, upon this very street, many times, and well into the dawn; and she would not deny you the fun, I am sure."

It was daylight, then, when I arrived back at Señorita Navarro's villa in Renata's carriage, and Auntie and her friend only smiled at me over the breakfast table as I came in. I am afraid that I slept away most of my first full day in Barcelona, but I would not have traded away even an hour of that night for a whole year of tomorrows, and when I finally put aside my party dress and crawled into the big bed, I slipped not only between the covers but into Renata's arms; and when I awoke at midday it was to the touch of her hands and shortly thereafter, to the touch of her tongue upon my most intimate places. And now I must finish my letter, Alicia, and prepare to post it and then to dress; for I have been told that there are more parties tonight, and it would not do to be late.

Your friend,
Elaine

"CARLY AND MARGOT"
(from *A Circle of Friends*)

Margot held her breath as Carly lifted up the tail of her loose knit shirt. This was always her very favorite part, when Carly's tits were exposed to her.

It wasn't just the tits themselves, although they were full and soft, perfect for squeezing and for playing with, for sucking into one's mouth and teasing with a tongue. What she loved were the tiny gold rings, one through each nipple, and the star and the moon indelibly cast into the skin above the right one. Margot, conservative and gentle, longed for such decorations on herself, but could not imagine lying still and actually having it done. Through Carly she got her chance to enjoy them fully.

She was so frequently dominated by other women, by strong women who bound her in wrist cuffs and strapped her creamy ass firmly with cruel leather paddles when she disobeyed them—or sometimes even when she did obey, just for the pleasure of the punishment. She enjoyed that, but she also enjoyed her relationship with Carly, both of them equal, both of them lovers. She took one of the nipple rings between her teeth. The brassy taste was almost sweet.

Margot was herself naked, and Carly reached out to take Margot's own nipples in her fingers. The two women were almost exact opposites. Margot was tall, willowy, fine-boned and fine-featured, her thick hair luxurious and long. Carly was much shorter, stockier, her breasts much fuller. Her hair was cut very short, almost shorn, and dyed red, at least at this particular moment. Each thoroughly enjoyed the contrast.

They were together in Carly's loft, one of the more eccentric places Margot had ever had reason to visit. Being an artist, Carly wanted to live in the manner that was expected of her. The difference was that she was a rather successful artist and had much more money at her disposal than most people in her profession. She also liked creature comforts, so she used her money to combine the austere artist's life with the luxuries she loved so much. Her loft consisted of the two upper floors of a huge warehouse. The walls were unfinished, sandblasted brick and exposed pipes, as most of the artists' lofts were. But Carly's floors were mirror-finished hardwood, her enormous bathroom contained a whirlpool bath, and most of the furniture was antique. That included her king-sized bed, a heavy brass frame with a canopy that held mosquito netting. Margot liked to be inside it, surrounded by the white gauze.

Right now, they were on the daybed, which was so

large that it was almost a double bed in itself. Carly had asked Margot to come up to her loft, and the young woman had torn herself away from her veterinary office as quickly as she could. On her own, her life was generally calm and orderly. In Carly she found a wild side that she felt was lacking in herself and she welcomed every opportunity to give in to it.

As for Carly, Margot was her calming effect. She enjoyed a wide range of lovers, most of them as outlandish as she. She enjoyed the company of dykes, which for her were the women who loved their sex hard and fast. With Margot she could be slow, gentle, romantic. The netting on the bed had been Margot's idea, taken from a magazine. Carly was now completely smitten with it and always slept inside its folds as if in the arms of a lover.

"I bought something yesterday," Carly said. It was almost a groan, for Margot's lips were still on her nipple, tugging gently at the gold ring.

"Do tell," Margot said in a muffled voice; her mouth never left the treat she had found.

"Let me go get it," Carly said, and tried to get up. Margot wouldn't let her. The tip of her tongue was now through the nipple ring, and her fingers were between Carly's legs. Carly was wet already, and Margot slipped a finger into the hot tunnel expertly.

The red-haired woman allowed Margot to push her back onto the daybed. The purchase could wait. Margot's long, slim fingers explored Carly's hot cunt eagerly until they were wet with pussyjuice, which Margot slowly sucked from them. Carly loved to watch her do that.

Carly felt like her whole pussy was liquid. Her skin seemed to mold itself to Margot's fingers, like she was sucking Margot's hand right up into herself. Now, bending over her, Margot was placing one well-formed breast between Carly's legs. She used the nipple to brush up and down on Carly's sex-swollen clit, to their mutual pleasure. The nipple slid over the wet pinkness as smoothly as a sigh.

"Your pussy is so beautiful," Margot said, as she moved her whole body back and forth to rub her tit on the sleek flesh. "I could sit here and play with it all day."

"You could," Carly sighed, "and I would let you. But I did buy something I think we can both have some fun with."

"In a minute," Margot said. "I can't stop now." She moved back between Carly's legs and with her hands, spread them apart even further. Then she put her head right beside that delicious cunt. The hair was trimmed and dyed the same outrageous shade of red as the hair on Carly's head. It was a game Carly played, and she had not forgotten the look on Margot's face when she had undressed in front of her several months ago. She had decided on a mixture of bright blue and yellow for her head, and had treated her pube to the same combination.

The color didn't matter at all right now. Margot had only one intention, and she snaked out her tongue to part the sweet lips and reach the treasure under them. It was honey sweet and hot as always. Margot wondered when there would be a tiny ring between these lips to tease with the tip of her tongue. It was something she had started longing for even if she didn't know exactly why.

Right now, though, everything she needed was here. She rimmed the entrance to Carly's hole with her tongue and then thrust it deep inside as if it were a kiss. Carly loved the full wet feeling and she pressed Margot into her. She wanted to swallow this woman whole.

She let Margot suck on her cunt for some time. The chills it sent through her were heavenly, but finally she could wait no longer to show off her purchase. She sat up and pulled Margot up to her, sharing a deep, rich kiss with the willowy woman as she did. Then she made her sit on the daybed while she went off to collect her delight, hidden under the bed, across the room.

She brought back the large box to the daybed, knelt on the thick Oriental carpet, and told Margot to close her eyes and not to peek while she opened the box.

Margot was completely taken when she was allowed to open her eyes again, and she just stared, her mouth open.

"It's a rider," Carly said, as she showed off the device.

That was certainly the word for it. It was a large, contoured cushion, meant to be straddled as it sat on the floor. What made it different was the accessory on it. Pointing up from the seat was a huge dildo.

Margot sat down on the floor and ran her hands over it. It had a thick knob on the top, which she felt all over with her fingers, and veins running through it so that it looked realistic. Both in length and width it was massive, and the soft plastic felt warm in her hands. It was certainly a toy to be reckoned with.

"It's amazing," she said. She couldn't take her fingers off the shaft that pointed up, begging for a pussy to sit on it.

"I've seen them in catalogues many times," Carly said. Like Margot, she couldn't keep her hands away from the amazing device. "When I was in the leather shop, I overheard someone ordering one and I knew I had to have one. I thought you'd appreciate it. I certainly know I will."

"Let me try it out," Margot said, getting up to put herself on the plastic knob.

Carly stopped her, a hand on her wrist. "Will you indulge me?"

Margot looked at her, puzzled, but she smiled broadly. "What's your pleasure?"

Carly looked almost bashful, a reaction Margot never thought she would see in her outgoing, outlandish lover. "When I got it, I could just see you sitting on it. I could just imagine the way you would take that knob into your pussy and move down on it until that shaft was all the way inside you."

"So what would you like?" Carly closed her eyes and breathed deeply; she wasn't gathering the nerve to ask the question, she was completely lost in the ecstasy of asking it. "I would like to shave you," she said. "I want to see it going into you completely naked. I want to see every movement, every touch of it on you."

She opened her eyes quickly. "Of course, if you don't want to—"

Margot smiled. "I hope you have plenty of shaving cream," she said. "There's nothing worse than getting nicked down there, I'm sure."

Carly led her to the bathroom. Margot was always amazed by this room, for it was so unlike anything she would expect to find in a loft. She had seen so many movies where the facilities in such an apartment consisted of a toilet and basin out in the open.

Carly, on the other hand, didn't see it that way. For

any crudeness she had elsewhere, she was very particular about her toilet habits and she had a passion for fancy bathrooms that few could match. She had spent a great deal of money, but she had exactly what she wanted.

It was a room of its own, huge, with a window that flooded the area with light. There was a copper-lined footed bathtub for long soaks and a shower with glass doors. There was a toilet and a bidet, and a sink set with a handmade enamel basin and elegant brass fittings. In one corner was the whirlpool bath with its delightful jets, which Margot had often pointed at her pussy with orgasmic results. The bathroom was so big that it held three chairs and a cupboard almost overflowing with thick bath sheets.

This was not a spur-of-the-moment question. On the table beside one of the chairs was a shaving kit, neatly set out. There was a mug of shaving cream and a brush, a comb, scissors, a razor and blades. The chair was protected by a thin plastic sheet and there was a bowl for warm water. Margot could imagine Carly getting everything ready. Indeed, while Carly had been setting it out—even including a linen napkin beneath everything on the table—the excitement had been enough to set her pussy throbbing and she had had to stop halfway through and use her fingers to make herself come.

Carly now sat Margot down in the chair, her legs spread wide, and almost reverently she kissed the hairy lips before she proceeded. First came the scissors, and she snipped the dark pubic hair away until only a short bristle remained. Margot was tense at first, but gradually she relaxed; she had complete faith in Carly's abilities with the scissors and the razor. The cold touch of the metal against her was exciting itself.

Now she took the brush and used it to whip the shaving cream in the mug. It was thick and rich and smelled almost spicy. She used the brush to mound the cream on Margot's pussy. It was warm and the brush tickled; Margot sighed and moved forward in the chair so that Carly could soap all of her.

Carly spent a long time doing this, for she loved the sight of Margot's pussy all fluffy and white with the thick cream. At one point she turned the brush around and probed into the white mound with the handle. Margot groaned as the ivory handle pushed against her clit. The shaving cream made her whole pussy tingle, a new and delightful experience. Even when it stung slightly on her clit, it was still a sweet sensation. She could imagine being completely covered in it, her whole body as white as her cunt.

She couldn't help tensing up at the first touch of the razor against her skin. Carly had warmed it in the water first, but there was still the involuntary reaction—this was a horrendously sharp steel blade taking the hair away from the most vulnerable part of her body. As with the scissors, though, the tension passed very quickly. A dominatrix might have nicked her just on principle. Carly, she knew, would not hurt her.

It was an unusual sensation. Carly used short strokes, cleaning the razor often. It was difficult to scrape the thick hair away and she had to pass over the skin several times until it was smooth. Margot could feel it, the razor catching on the hairs at first, and then eventually gliding over the skin. She looked down. Carly had cleaned all of the hair off her mound and was working her way down to the cream-covered lips. The skin was pale and it looked unusual without the hair, but the sight of it excited Margot as much as it did Carly. She had never been shaved before. It would be a new experience for them both.

It was much more difficult to take the razor over the curves and folds of Margot's pussylips. Carly worked at it slowly, carefully. She used her fingers to stretch the skin and Margot sighed at the touch on this most sensitive area. The contrast between Carly's warm hands and the cool razor was intoxicating. Even the inherent danger of the sharp blade excited her.

When Margot's cuntlips were silky smooth, Carly shaved the insides of her thighs and all the way down to her sweet asshole, should any stray hairs be lurking there. When the job was finished, she took a thick towel and wiped away the last of the shaving cream, then she gave Margot a hand mirror so that she might admire the job.

Margot couldn't stop looking. She had never seen herself this way before, so young looking, so clean, so smooth. She held the lips together until her pussy was just a straight line between her legs. Then she spread it with her fingers and admired her large clit and the inner folds that were exposed. Her own touch on her skin was magical. Without any hair in the way she felt completely naked.

Carly finished the job by using her tongue on this newly shaved area. Margot almost cried out. It was unlike any tonguing she had ever received before. There was no barrier, just hot tongue on hot cunt, smooth mouth on hairless pussy. She almost came with just a few long, slow laps.

Carly wasn't about to give in that easily, though. "Come on," she said, taking Margot's hand. "We have a toy to play with, remember?"

In the excitement of the shaving Margot had completely forgotten Carly's "rider." Now she felt as if she were a different woman approaching it. The first time she had been a novice. This time she had been carefully prepared for what was to come. She thought of herself almost like a bride dressed and preened for the occasion, being led toward her wedding night.

Carly sank to the floor beside the device and touched her tongue to the tip of the knob. Margot watched, wanting her desperately as she did. Carly sucked it for Margot's benefit, wrapping her tongue around the shaft and taking it into her mouth.

"Suck it off!" Margot whispered, kneeling down on the thick carpet beside her. "Suck it off like you want to make it come." Carly began serious sucking on the monstrous dick. Margot wrapped her hand around the base of it, and with her other hand, played with the rings in Carly's nipples. She couldn't keep her eyes off Carly and the dildo in her mouth. Carly, meanwhile, kept glancing admiringly at Margot's sweet hairless cunt. She had had hairless women before, many times, but she had never actually shaved anyone before. It was sweet to look at her own handiwork.

The dildo was now glistening wet with saliva. Margot put her hand between her legs and felt the smooth slit there. Her pussy was soaked and she sat back and spread her legs so that Carly could see. She took her fingers, wet with cuntjuice, and rubbed the juice onto her pussylips until the whole area was shiny. Without any hair in the way, Carly got the full effect of drenched lips and the sweet slit that had provided the nectar. She breathed deeply and sucked the knob into her mouth.

"I'm wet," Margot said, "and I'm ready for it. Can I play with your toy?"

Carly moved back and indicated the rubber prick standing at attention. "Be my guest," she said.

Margot squatted over the dildo and used her fingers to spread her lips wide. The opening to her tunnel was clearly visible, hairless, waiting. Carly was bending down now, looking up at Margot from underneath so that she could see everything.

The plastic knob waited patiently. Margot moved down so that her pussylips were just touching it. Then she swung her hips back and forth, rubbing the whole length of her slit on the huge toy. A fine string of pussyjuice stretched from Margot's cunt to the knob as she did. Carly was transfixed. The juice on the head looked thick and creamy and had the lovely honey smell of Margot's cunt. Carly could almost imagine it slowly running down the shaft like a sweet liqueur.

Margot was achingly slow, prolonging both her own pleasure and Carly's, for both of them were enjoying this gorgeous woman atop the rubber pleasure-giver. The pink plastic was almost ruby against the stark creaminess of Margot's newly sheared mound. Her lips opened to accept the head and Margot paused with the tip right at the entrance to her tunnel. Then she moved ever so slightly, and the smooth head disappeared into the delicious crack.

Carly used her fingers to pull Margot's lips apart so that she could see her lover fill up with the dildo. Margot pushed herself down on it slowly, slowly, groaning as the rubber prick opened her to gain access. When all of the head was engulfed, she fucked it. It popped out, naked and shiny for just a moment, and then was taken back into that hot cave. It was an amazing sight. All of Margot's pussy spread to take it in, and then when the head was completely inside, the lips closed around the glans and held it firmly.

Now Margot took the device in deeper. She wanted

to stay just on the head of it, teasing Carly with her shaved pussy, but it felt too good to have her cunt filled. She moved up and down on it, each time moving further down. The shaft, when she lifted herself up, was shiny with her juice.

Carly had an inspiration, and she got up, kissing Margot firmly before she left to go into the bathroom. When she came back, she had the hand mirror she had used to show Margot her new nakedness. Now she knelt on the floor in front of the rider and positioned the mirror so that Margot could see everything that was going on.

Margot was fascinated. Her shaved pussy looked delightful impaled on the dildo. Slowly she lifted herself up the whole length of the shaft. Her pussylips stretched down on it, as if trying to keep it inside. She played for a while with the head right at the entrance to her hole, then she sank down on it, watching the hairless lips fold inward to accept its massive width and length. Her groan was both for the sight of it and for the delicious fullness it produced.

"Now fuck it!" Carly said. One hand held the mirror, the other was among her bright red pubic hair, playing with her clit. "You love it, don't you? Show it! Fuck that prick hard!"

Margot couldn't do anything less. She was on fire now with her cunt so full. She had the dildo in completely and her ass was smacking against the cushion she was squatting on. She was riding it now. She discovered that in front of the dildo there was an area covered in soft, rubbery bumps. This was right where her clit came down and the bumps, like tiny fingers, massaged her sweetly distended button each time she slammed down on the dick. Each touch sent shivers through her.

Margot was fucking it as hard as she could now. Carly loved the sound of her asscheeks as they slapped against the rider. Margot's hair was flying wildly and her eyes were tightly closed. She was whispering, "Fuck me, fuck me, fuck me," like a chant, barely aware that she was doing it. Only one thing mattered to her now, and that was her enjoyment on this amazing device.

Carly, watching her, now had put the mirror down, and moved both hands between her legs. One was massaging her throbbing clit while the other was thrust firmly into her vagina, pushing in and out. The rhythm of her fingers in her cunt matched Margot's on the riding dildo. Not even touching, they were still fucking together.

Margot was bouncing on the device. Her tits moved with her and she reached down to take her nipples between her fingertips and squeeze them. She stretched them out, tweaking them, and groaned at the thrills she was giving herself. Her whole body was soaked with sex.

"Fuck it hard, Margot!" Carly whispered. She was giving it to herself just as hard with her fingers, and her other hand was almost pounding on her clit. Pushing it back and forth, up and down, she brought herself closer and closer to her goal.

"So hard!" Margot gasped in agreement. She was filled with the dildo and the rubber bumps were pounding on her clit. She had her tits stretched out, her fingers on her nipples and twisting them. Finally she felt as if she was at the crest of a great hill. She let herself go over the top of it, and fell long and deep into her orgasm.

When she saw Margot coming, Carly let herself go

too. Hands working frantically in her cunt, she brought on her own climax, and side by side, the two rode out their peaks until both were spent.

Gasping, Margot slowed down and finally stopped. She was hunkered down on the rider, and the entire length of the thick shaft was still inside her steamy tunnel. By moving back and forth, she drained the last few shivers out and then slowly dismounted.

The shaft was soaked with her juice. With an almost overwhelming longing, Carly leaned over and licked it off. It was as rich and sweet as she had imagined. She couldn't stop until the whole device was clean. Then she kissed Margot deeply, who greedily sucked the taste of her own pussy from the tongue of her lover.

Somewhat shaky, they managed to get up to the daybed, where they collapsed beside each other. Margot was still breathing hard and Carly was savoring the taste that lingered on her lips and tongue. She couldn't get enough of it.

Idly she ran her fingers over Margot's shorn pussy. The skin above her slit was so smooth it felt slippery even though it was dry. Her lips were still soaked, though, and Carly ran her finger over them and sucked the juice off, over and over, until the skin was clean. The gesture reminded Margot of someone cleaning a plate to get the last bit of chocolate sauce. For Carly, the thick nectar was just as sweet and just as desirable.

Once that was done, Carly's hand was replaced by Margot's own. Her shaved pussy felt so unusual and she just had to touch it. The skin seemed hotter than it ever had been, almost feverish, and as smooth as anything she could imagine. The cleft of her pussy and her lips felt so foreign without their hair and yet so familiar. She knew she would be reaching for it many times in the days to come, for it was so new and exciting.

"I've had my pussy shaved clean before," Carly said. "When it grows back it's going to itch like crazy."

"I kind of expected that," Margot said. Her fingers in her cunt were beginning to excite her again. "What's the best thing for it?"

Carly winked at her. "Shaving it again," she said. She had been so taken with the whole experience, she longed for the next time she could put out the razor and the mug carefully on the linen napkin and use the brush to whip up the thick cream to coat Margot's pussy again.

"I might just have to do that," Margot said. "How soon before I'll need another?"

"A week or so."

"And any volunteers?"

Carly laid back, closed her eyes and smiled. "Now what do you think?"

"FOR ONE NIGHT ONLY"
(from *Provincetown Summer & Other Stories*)

In Colorado, the mountains that so overwhelm visitors to the state become as natural to the residents as rain or snow. So I've been told, but even after almost eight years of living in Aspen, I still marveled at them each time I went outside. Lushly green in summer or mounded white in winter, they rose up majestically on either side of the town. Their peaks always reminded me of a woman's breasts, which could be why they held such fascination for me.

The fascination had been enough for me to arrive in Aspen for a ski trip and decide, on a moment's notice, that the flat lands back at the coast were no longer what I wanted. I moved to Aspen and eventually opened a women's clothing store in the heart of the town's shopping district. Not only did it generate enough for me to live comfortably, but it was small enough that I was able to run it myself.

Although the taller peaks were still snow-capped, the June morning was sunny and warm as I locked my front door and walked to my store. Aspen attracts tourists all year round, and I was glad to see that many of the cars parked by the sidewalk had out-of-state plates. Visitors generated most of my sales.

I stopped at the bakery near my store to pick up a coffee and muffin to take with me. "Morning, Lucy!" I called to the owner, as I poured a cup of steaming coffee.

She turned around from the oven, where she was arranging pans of bread dough. "Morning, Amy," she smiled. "You're up bright and early today."

"Figure it's the only way I can guarantee getting anything," I replied. Within the hour, Lucy's bakery would be packed with people. I had learned to get up a little earlier to beat the crowd.

It also gave me a chance to talk to Lucy, who worked long hours and didn't have a lot of time to socialize. When we discovered we were both lesbian, we naturally seemed to open up to each other, and this in turn led to a firm friendship. We had never been lovers; although we never discussed it, we both seemed to prefer a platonic relationship. It just was wonderful to have a friend who thought the same way, who shared my outlooks and concerns. On the occasional evening we got together for drinks at the bar down the street from my store.

"I just took those blueberry ones out of the oven," she said, and I picked up one of the huge muffins. It was still warm and fragrant. I put it in a bag myself, as all of Lucy's regular customers did, and left the money on the counter by the cash register.

The bread in the oven, she turned to me, wiping her floury hands on a cloth. "It's going to be pretty busy today," she said. "I've got two extra batches of bread made, and extra pies. You've got it lucky, girl. All you have to do is show people where the zipper is!"

I laughed. "I expect to be run off my feet too, today," I said. A large convention was being held in one of the resort lodges in Aspen over the next four days, and almost every hotel room in the town was booked. Aspen was a small town, with most of its stores clustered together. Tourists generally walked through all of it, stopping in each store. The merchants were quite pleased with the convention, and a lot of stores were already noticing extra sales from people who had arrived a day early.

"At least you just sell the clothes, you can't have to sew them up too!" Lucy laughed. "I've been baking since three this morning. Tell you what, though. When this crowd goes home, we'll get together and treat ourselves to a nice dinner out. What do you say?"

"You're on," I said, picking up a napkin and heading for the door. "Let me know when you're free."

It felt good to unlock the front door of my shop. It gave me great satisfaction knowing that I had done it all myself and had made a pretty good business out of it. I locked the door behind me, and went back to my little office to enjoy my coffee and muffin in peace.

By opening time everything was arranged. In the front window I had some hand-painted shirts and scarves dyed to look like Navajo blankets. Belts adorned with silver and turquoise hung near the door, with beaded moccasins below on a rack. I had long ago learned to lure tourists into the shop with clothes they couldn't buy at home, and these were my most popular items.

At nine o'clock I opened the front door and used a battered corn broom to sweep the sidewalk outside the window. Other shopkeepers up and down the street were doing the same thing, and we called good mornings to each other.

Most of the day the store enjoyed a steady stream of customers. It was obvious the convention wrapped up for the day around three, for the sidewalks were packed with people in the late afternoon and I was almost run off my feet with customers, just as I had told Lucy. As I expected, my window displays were very effective and I managed to sell a large number of the expensive hand-painted shirts and the decorated belts.

Business died down around six, and now it was time for me to take a breather while the restaurants scurried to keep up with the crowds. My store was empty for the first time and I took advantage of it to unwrap the sandwich I had bought earlier in the day.

I only got a couple of bites when a woman walked in. I could only stare. She was gorgeous. She had a model's face, or a movie star's, with fine features and enormous brown eyes. Her hair was carefully arranged and she was expensively dressed. I wanted her as soon as I laid eyes on her. She was so sensuous, so graceful.

My sandwich was forgotten. "Are you looking for anything specific?" I asked, as she looked over a rack of shirts by the window.

She turned to me. Was I imagining it, or did I catch a spark in her eyes? "I'm looking for a dress," she said. "A summery one, something light."

I led her to the back of the store where the dresses

were. I could smell her perfume and I wanted to touch her hair. My pussy was stirring as I looked her over, trying to decide on which style I should show her.

"How about this?" I asked. I pulled out a rich red dress that would show off her breasts. "Or maybe something shorter?" I found a lovely purple one.

"Let me try the red one," she said, smiling at me. I showed her where the fitting room was. She disappeared inside. I wished I could have gone with her to help her undress.

She came out shortly in the bright red dress. As I expected, it hung perfectly on her. It was low in front and the tops of her creamy breasts were so inviting.

"That is gorgeous!" I said, as she moved in front of the full-length mirror. It really did suit her, and she knew it. She caught my eyes in the mirror and again smiled at me.

She turned around to face me, and tugged at the neckline. "Do you think this sits right?" she asked. "Is this how it's supposed to fit?"

I reached for the fabric. "That's the way—" I stopped. She had leaned into me, so that my hand pressed against her warm breast. "Oh—excuse me," I said.

"No need to," she smiled. She looked again in the mirror. "You're right, it's perfect. I'll take it."

She went back into the changing room. I didn't know what to think. She had obviously gone out of her way to set me up and push against me. I could still feel her body against my hand, and the sensation made my pussy tingle. I didn't dare believe that she wanted me, but I wished with all my heart that she did.

She came out, and I took the dress to the counter and began to wrap it in tissue paper.

"Are you here for the convention?" I asked.

"Only for today," she said. "I had to give a seminar, but I have to be back in New York tomorrow morning. It's a shame, really. This is a beautiful place and I wish I could stay longer and see it."

I slipped the dress inside a bag. She handed over her credit card. Sharon MacMillan. I wanted to speak her name, to whisper in her ear.

"So," she said, "what do people do in this town for excitement on a Thursday night?"

"Well, there's a lot of good restaurants, and there's live entertainment in the lounge down the street," I said.

She glanced around to be sure the store was empty, then leaned toward me. "Maybe you'd like to show me around. After all, I'm only here for one night."

My heart was beating so hard I thought she could hear it. Although I wanted her, I suddenly found myself as flustered as a schoolgirl at her boldness. "I don't close the shop until nine o'clock," I stammered.

She was cool as could be, and I envied her and wanted her both at the same time. "Then I'll be back at nine," she said. "You look like the type who could show a lady a good time—are you?"

"Yes," I said, almost in a whisper. Then to my surprise, she picked up the bag, leaned over the counter and kissed me on the lips. I was shocked at first, but in seconds I was returning it. Her lips were warm and smooth, and her tongue darted out to tease mine ever so gently. Then she stood up straight.

"Nine o'clock," she promised, and left the store.

I went limp with desire. This was the sort of thing I

read in magazines! But here it was, happening to me, right in my own store. My pussy was throbbing so badly I couldn't stand it. I rushed and locked the door.

I hurried into the changing room. I just couldn't bear the unsatisfied heat any longer. I pulled up my skirt and slipped off my panties. Sitting in the chair, facing the mirror, I saw my wet pussy. My hand was on my clit in seconds. Each flick of my finger was Sharon's tongue massaging my hot cunt lips. I slipped a finger inside my wet hole, and imagined that it was her finger feeling me up. My tongue darted in my mouth. I wanted to lick her pussy so badly I could almost taste it.

I watched myself in the mirror as I rubbed my pussy. My fingers were wet with my hot juice and they looked so good against the dark hair. My hand went up to hold my breast and twist the nipple through my shirt. I could feel her hands on them. I wanted to feel her hands on my cunt.

Normally I teased myself and took a long time when I made myself come. Now I was so horny I couldn't wait. My clit was so hard and rubbing it felt so good. My nipples were erect and I could see them through my shirt. I pulled them hard, gasping at how delicious it felt.

I rubbed harder and faster. I worked myself up to an edge, then let myself fall over it into my orgasm. It was wonderful. I fingered myself until the last of it was finished. I sat for a few moments to collect myself, then I straightened my dress and went back to open the store.

I went through the rest of the day almost in a dream. I had never been approached in such a way before. Sharon's shameless advances had turned me on. And that saucy kiss! No one had ever done that before. This was a very strong woman, one who would control me, and the idea was exciting. I longed to melt in her arms and let her do with me whatever she wanted.

At eight thirty I decided to close up early, the first time I had ever done so. I then went back into the shop and went through the racks of dresses. I found one that had just come in the week before, a beautiful pale silk one. I tried it on. It fit perfectly and I thought it was stunning. I hung up my own dress in the back room, fixed my hair, and decided I would worry about accounting for the dress in the stock books tomorrow.

At nine o'clock I heard a tapping at the glass door. Sharon was right on time. She was dressed in a softly tailored suit that showed off her beautiful body to full advantage. I opened the door and she walked into the store.

"You look lovely," she said. "Are you closed for the night? Good, let's go get something to eat. I'm starving."

I suggested a restaurant on the next block, and she agreed. The night was pleasantly warm and we walked over.

The restaurant was dark and quiet. We were led to a table by the window, where we could watch people walking by and see the mountains that rose up at the edge of town.

We both ordered cocktails, and the server brought us a menu. When it arrived, Sharon lifted her glass in a toast. "I'm glad I met you today," she said. "I'm usually lost in the evenings when I have to go on business trips. This is so pleasant."

"It's a nice change for me, too," I admitted. "I

usually just go home and stick some dinner in the microwave, then go to bed with a book. It's nice to have my own store, but it sure means long hours."

We ordered dinner, and Sharon asked for a bottle of wine. She sat back and looked out the window. "I've never been in Colorado before," she said. "This is a beautiful place. I can understand why you live here."

"Where are you staying?" I asked.

"At a lodge just outside of town," she said. "Have you ever been inside it?" I admitted I hadn't.

She reached over and put her hand on mine. Her soft touch sent ripples through me. "Then you must come back with me and see it," she said. "I'm only here for tonight. You may not get the chance again."

My pussy was burning. I hardly even noticed what my appetizer was. All I saw were Sharon's rich, full lips and her soft hands. I wanted them on my body, and it looked as if I was going to get my wish.

She definitely wasn't subtle. Putting down her fork, she leaned across the table and looked deep into my eyes. "I want you," she said.

"I was hoping you would," I whispered. "I think you're beautiful."

She smiled. "Then let's enjoy our dinner," she said. "Fine dining is a sensual experience too. Then we can go back to my room for dessert."

She was definitely a connoisseur. The wine she had ordered matched perfectly with our food, which the restaurant had prepared in its usual impeccable style. Sharon was impressed with the quality, and admitted that it rivaled some of the finer restaurants she frequented in New York. It filled me with pride to hear her say that.

Our evening decided, Sharon switched the conversation easily. She asked about the store and my lifestyle in Aspen, and seemed genuinely interested in my answers. She told me she was a consultant for a large New York computer firm, which not only accounted for her hectic business trips but also for the fact that she refused to let me pay anything for the expensive dinner.

I enjoyed her company immensely. The time flew by, and before I knew it, it was eleven o'clock. When our coffee was finished, she asked if I was still interested in seeing her room. What a question! My pussy had been on fire throughout the entire dinner.

We walked back to my store. Sharon's car, a rented Cadillac sedan, was parked in front. It was quite a switch from my little Chevy, and I stretched out on the comfortable seat.

Within minutes we were outside of Aspen. The lodge was a beautiful one, tucked up at the base of the mountain for skiing in winter. At the front door, the valet held the car doors open for us, then got in himself and drove it away.

The front lobby was beautifully decorated, but that wasn't what I wanted to see. We went up on the elevator, and I waited while Sharon opened the door to her room.

Sharon must have been as hot as I was. As soon as she closed the door behind us, I found myself in her arms, her mouth on mine. It felt so good to let myself go. I returned her kiss. She pressed her tongue inside my mouth, and my own rose to meet it. My pussy was already wet as she ran her hands down my neck and held my breasts through my dress.

I reached for hers. They were firm and felt heavy in

my hands. She kissed me for what seemed like hours. Her mouth was sweet and her kisses were like honey. Her tongue moved so beautifully in my mouth I thought that she might be able to make me come just like that.

Finally she stepped back and began to unbutton my dress. I reached for her, but she gently pushed my hands down. "Let me," she said. "You just relax. I want to make love to you."

She pushed the dress off my shoulders and it fell to the floor. "You are exquisite," she said, and bent down to nibble at my breasts through my bra. Once again she would not let me raise my hands. I could only stand there and enjoy everything she was doing to me.

She kissed me deeply as she reached around my back to unhook my bra. She murmured approval, and immediately bent down and licked my nipple. I moaned. Her mouth was just as I had imagined it would be. My pussy was now throbbing hard and I longed for relief.

She turned me around and lowered me onto the bed. "I love your tits!" she whispered and showed her appreciation. I had never had such attention lavished on them. She ran her hands under them and pushed them together, then sucked my nipples into her mouth and licked the tips of them. She rubbed her own nipples over them, through her clothes. She tickled them with her hair, and blew gently on them to cool them off. Then she took them into her warm mouth. That made me groan with pleasure.

"Please let me see you," I begged. She sucked my nipples for a little while longer, then stood up. She took her clothes off slowly. Her body was magnificent.

She really did look like a model with her firm breasts and slim waist. Her pussy was dark and I wanted more than anything to put my tongue in between her hairy lips. She even surprised me with a tiny butterfly tattoo on her hip.

She then returned to me. It turned her on to give me pleasure and she did a beautiful job. She made me roll over, and she ran her fingernails up and down my back for a long time. Then she used her tongue, moving slowly down my body until she reached my ass. Here she used her tongue to tease me, flicking it between my cheeks while she kneaded my ass with her fingers. I could only lie on the bed and soak up her attention. It was wonderful beyond comprehension.

"Roll over," she said, and I was only too happy to. Again she used her tongue to draw long strokes on my body, from my breasts down to my belly. I was getting hotter and hotter as she moved closer to my soaked pussy.

My hands moved up to touch her, but each time she gently put them back at my sides. "Just enjoy it," she said. "You'll get your turn later."

It was easy to enjoy what she was doing. She licked down to my hair, then went right around my throbbing pussy and licked the insides of my thighs. It was heavenly. Her touch was so soft as she thrilled me with her mouth.

Her first flick across my clit made me gasp. She licked me slowly the whole length of my pussy. I shivered and moaned as she stroked my clit with just the tip of her tongue.

She licked her finger, then slowly pushed it into my hole. The lubrication wasn't necessary. I was so wet I could feel my hot juice on the insides of my thighs.

She slowly fucked me with one finger, then two. It was a wonderful full feeling, and even better when she went back to licking my clit as she pushed her fingers inside.

"Tell me how good it feels," she said. "I like to hear what you're feeling." She pushed her tongue under the folds of my pussy lips and ran it around the top of my cunt.

"It feels so good!" I gasped. "Your tongue—right there! Oh yes, lick me on that spot!"

"Tell me about it," she said. She slipped her hand down to tickle at my ass. I couldn't stop my hips from moving.

"It feels so warm," I said. It really did, both the warmth from her wet tongue and the heat that was constantly building up inside me. "It's so warm, and it's just like all of you is inside me!"

She teased me. She would suck hard at my clit for a while until I got close to coming, then back off and lap slowly. The buildup was beautiful.

"Would you like to come now?" she asked. I was so worked up I could only nod, and I felt her tongue move up my pussy to my clit.

Her tongue moved so fast I couldn't believe it. I got closer and closer and then without warning the cascade started in my cunt and flooded over me. Still I wanted more, and she didn't stop. Within a few seconds, a second wave filled me and I cried out. It was so intense! My whole body was on fire as she licked the last few shivers out of me.

She stretched out beside me, idly drawing circles around my nipple with her fingernail. "It was nice, wasn't it?" she purred. I could only whisper a yes; I was still coming down from my explosive orgasm. "I knew it would be." She bent down and kissed my lips.

In one swift move she was over me, straddling my face with her beautiful pussy. I had waited so long for this. I could smell her lovely aroma and see the glistening lips. "Bring it down to me," I begged. "Let me lick your pussy!"

She did. Her cunt was rich and sweet. I held her ass cheeks and kneaded them while my tongue danced over her clit. I pulled her down so that my tongue fitted into her hole, and fucked her with it. My whole face was wet with her honey.

She moaned as I flitted over her pussy. I tried to be as slow and teasing as she had been with me, but it was impossible. She was going wild on my tongue. She moved her hips and ground her sweet pussy on my mouth. I ate her furiously. I loved having her cunt right on my face and her clit in my mouth.

"Lick me harder!" she begged. I concentrated all of my efforts on the hard nub of flesh. She began to moan, then gasped and cried out as she came. I was buried in her pussy. She trembled for a long time and I licked slowly at her until she finally got up and lay down beside me.

"Wonderful," she gasped, and kissed me again. "That was just fantastic." I ran my hands up and down her firm body and hugged her tightly.

We held each other for a long time. She reached up and smoothed my hair back from my face and gently kissed my cheek and eyelids. "I'm so glad I ran into you today," she said. "I haven't had anything that nice for so long."

"I haven't either," I said. "No one's ever eaten me like that before."

She kissed me again. "I have to be up at five to catch

my plane," she said. "I can take you back to your house and you'll have lots of time to open your store. Will you please stay the night with me?"

Would I! I felt so satisfied and content, I couldn't imagine getting up and leaving. "Of course," I said. Sharon motioned for me to move so that she could pull the covers up over ourselves. I snuggled into her arms and we spent another hour just talking.

"I wish I didn't have to go so soon," she said. "I'd really like to get to know you better."

"I'm always here," I said. "You know where my store is. I'm sure you'll be back for another meeting sometime."

She smiled. "If not, then I guess I could always learn to ski. It would be a perfect excuse for a trip."

Finally she turned the light out. I fell into such a deep sleep it seemed like only minutes before the wake-up call disturbed us. Sharon kissed me and we dressed and went downstairs to where the car was waiting at the front door.

She drove me into town and stopped in front of my house. The street was still empty at that early hour.

She leaned over and kissed me, a long, gentle kiss. "I only wish we could have had more time," she said.

"So do I," I said. "It really was wonderful."

She reached into her pocket and pulled out a business card. "I'm definitely going to try to get back here soon," she said. "In the meantime, if you come out New York way, please let me know." I promised I would.

Reluctantly I got out of the car and closed the door. There was one last look, and then she pulled away from the curb. I watched the car until she finally turned the corner out of sight.

Back to my regular routine. I went in the house, showered and dressed, and watered the plants. Then I grabbed my bag and began my familiar route to work.

Lucy was making rolls in the empty bakery. I let the wooden screen door slam, as I always did, and called out my good morning as I reached for a cup and the pot of coffee.

"Morning, Amy!" she called out. "So what's new with you?"

I put the coffee pot back on the burner, then leaned over the counter and took a sip. "Lucy," I began, "you wouldn't believe it."

"MISTRESS LYLA"
(from *Necessary Evil*)

"Sure is hot," the woman says as she passes on the street. "It is," I reply. It's only the type of pleasantry strangers exchange when they meet, but today it's a very accurate one. I'm back in the land of Southern hospitality and the thermometer is snaking very close to the top on this stifling, humid day.

I am also back with my Southern Mistress, who has called me and told me to come to her house. It is the first time I have seen her since we came back from Toronto, six days ago. The first sound of her voice on the phone made me weak.

How I remember that trip! As tired as I was, there was little sleep for me that first night. My arms and legs alternated between cramps and numbness, firmly attached to each other by the plastic straps.

I would force myself to calm down, listening to my

Mistress's slow, even breathing as she lay in the comfortable bed above me. After a while I would doze off, but it would either be a light, twilight sleep from which I easily awoke or a deeper sleep with frightening dreams that would rouse me. The first time I came out of a dream, I momentarily forgot where I was, and I thrashed about until I realized why I could not move. The straps cut painfully into my wrists and ankles.

I was powerless to even roll over onto my other side, and my ribs and hips began to ache from lying on the floor. No carpet, no matter how thick, can protect a slave when her superior decides that the floor will make an adequate bed.

I believe at one point I began to sob, but only part of it was because of my agony. It felt so fulfilling to be there, under my Mistress's command. It was something my former Mistress Laura would never have thought of, and it made me so much happier to know that my decision about my co-worker Lyla Kirk had been the right one.

Halfway through the night, something happened that made me think about it even more. Waking up from yet another dream, I pulled hard against the plastic straps, which did not give.

I realized then that, for the first time, my Mistress had put me into bonds that I could not possibly escape from. Our company makes these tie-wraps to be the best and strongest on the market, and they are. The plastic straps can be broken, but only by someone with much, much more strength than I, and my wrists would probably snap before the restraints would.

Up until that point, my Mistress had doled out punishments that I had to choose to accept as they were handed out: I could have unbuckled the wrist cuffs or walked away from the paddle, if I had chosen to do so. But from this torture there was no escape. I was completely in her control. She could get up in the morning, get dressed and depart, leaving me completely helpless to be found by the maid. I would not be able to leave this room, stand up or even stretch my limbs unless my Mistress cut the straps.

That filled my heart until I thought it would burst, and it was the revelation I needed. I loved her so much at that point I could hardly wait until morning just to see her face. Sleep still did not come easily, but I spent the rest of the night contented.

The morning at the trade show was another story. It was some time before my cramped legs would even hold me up, and I hurt right through to my bones. Fortunately my Mistress allowed me the pleasure of a long, hot shower—providing I licked her pussy, which took no urging at all—and I stood under the steaming water until my muscles loosened. Struggling in the straps had left dark marks on my wrists and ankles, and I was thankful that I had included a long-sleeved shirt in my suitcase.

Cleo noticed right away. "What happened to you?" she asked, as soon as we were alone together. I was still walking stiffly and this, combined with the shirt, caught her attention.

I told her everything that had happened, and vicariously she drank it all in. I could imagine how wet her pussy was getting as I recounted the story, for I knew just how soaked mine was getting! I forgot my discomfort momentarily when we got busy at the booth, but whenever there was a lull, I relaxed long enough to notice just how sore I really was.

Mistress Lyla spent much of the day going around to other booths to see how they were set up and how their representatives worked with the clients. Occasionally she would come back to our booth, often with coffee for both of us, and when she looked at me I thought I would melt. I slept on the floor every night after that, in different configurations. One night she put the leather cuffs on me and snapped them together, so that I could move my legs but had to keep my wrists together. Another night I had one wrist shackled to one ankle. Each morning, Cleo looked at my stiff walk and sighed longingly.

The bag from the leather shop remained by my Mistress's suitcase, obviously still containing items that I had not seen. My whole being strained to open the top and look inside, but I dared not, and I still do not know what else was inside.

There are two trucks in Mistress Lyla's driveway, both with the name of a well-known contractor painted on the side. As I walk up to the house I hear hammering and turn to see men working at the garage.

They look at me, appraising me. They are good-looking men, well tanned and muscled from working in the sun, but they do not interest me. I am here for one reason only, and that is my Mistress Lyla. The men go back to work, carrying items into the large garage, and I continue on to the house.

"You look hot," my Mistress says, as she opens the door for me. "It is very warm outside, Mistress," I say. I feel sodden. My dress is wet and my hair is limp, and the cool air of her house is as refreshing as a tall drink. She is impeccable, fresh and crisp in her linen dress, and I feel grimy next to her.

"It must be hot working in that garage," she says, as she looks out the front door to see what is progressing. "Well, I'm paying to have it renovated, and the weather is not my problem." She closes the door behind us. I wonder if the men working out there could have any clue as to the special relationship that will be played out in this house.

"Naked, please," she says almost absently. It is the way she prefers me to be, and indeed it is the way I prefer it myself. I have taken to wearing nothing but thin dresses with nothing underneath, so that I can shed my clothes almost immediately. I do this now and stand before her, completely naked. I marvel that she practically ignores the fact that a nude woman is before her, ready for her commands. I know that I could never be a Mistress; this haughty, elegant, necessary detachment would be beyond me. She, instead, has grown into it and has made it a second skin.

She, on the other hand, wears a gorgeous set of silk lounging pajamas, obviously expensive and very suited to her. She has an iced coffee in one hand, and it thrills me to see her like this. She is my Southern plantation owner, my Mistress, my superior. She lives the life of leisure, and I am her property, bound to obey her commands.

"It occurred to me," she says, "that the fact that you like to be ordered to do things could prove useful to me."

"Mistress?" I ask.

"Well," she says, "I have been doing a bit of research and I've discovered that domination doesn't always have to be directly sexual. Am I correct?"

"Absolutely, Mistress," I reply. How else can I

explain it? Everything I do for my Mistress is done for sex and for love of her, even if it doesn't always involve tongues, pussies, fingers, and toys!

"I thought so," she says. "So I thought, why on earth am I paying a maid to come in and clean this house? I can save my money and just order my slave to do it."

"Mistress," I sigh, "tell me where the broom is." She is obviously delighted with this aspect of our roles as she points out the bucket, the mop, the dusters. "I don't expect you require constant supervision," she says.

"Mistress, you have commanded me to clean this house," I tell her. I know that my love for her shines in my eyes. "It will be spotless. As your submissive I can do no less."

"Then I have better things to do with my time than watch you sweep," she says, and she leaves the room. I breathe deeply, catching the last whiff of her cologne as she exits. I can hear her open the front door and as I glance down the hall, I see her looking out from the porch. She is obviously watching the men at work on her garage. I wonder idly what could possibly be done to renovate a garage; for a moment I imagine that she is thinking how nice it would be if she could simply order them to do their work just for the love of being commanded!

I only realize just how big this house is when I start to clean it. The kitchen floor is immense, all beautiful, cool, terra-cotta tile, and it doesn't take me long to mop it all down. But then I move through the long halls, into the enormous rooms, all of them done in hardwood floors with mats or small carpets on them. Three hours later, I have only done half of the main floor and there is still the floor above. Occasionally I can hear my Mistress, either her footsteps in the hallway above me or her voice coming from her chair on the porch as she talks on the phone. She does not come in, which makes me even more determined to do a perfect job. I feel a need to prove to her that I don't need her standing over me in order to have her commands carried out.

I am almost finished in the living room when I notice an unruly pile of books and papers on one table. I go to straighten it up and stop right in my tracks when I see what is on top.

It is a novel about submission, one of my favorites. I remember so well the night Cleo and I read it aloud to each other, stopping every chapter to relieve the pressure in our aching pussies. Now everything makes sense.

I open the book and thumb the pages I know so well. Sure enough, in chapter eight, the dominatrix orders her submissive to clean the house for her, since it doesn't make sense to pay a housekeeper. The submissive, ordered to remove her clothes, cleans the house in the nude. The book even contains the line my Mistress used—"I have better things to do with my time than watch you sweep!" No wonder it sounded so familiar!

I feel completely satisfied and almost subconsciously I hold the book to my chest. My Mistress has gone to the trouble of locating and reading books about domination and is using them like textbooks in order to learn exactly what she should do. She wants this just as much as I do.

I tidy the books, leaving them in the order they were in. Then, the room finished, I go back to the long hallway. The staircase rises majestically in front of me, but right now, all I can think about is how many risers there are to clean.

There is only one way to do them, and that is on my hands and knees, wiping each one down with oil soap. I am halfway up them when my Mistress's voice comes from behind me, saying, "You don't have to wax them, Jennifer. They're too slippery if you do."

"Thank you, Mistress," I say. I am very grateful for this. I am thrilled to be doing this under my Mistress's command, but to be truthful, I really don't enjoy housecleaning at all, and I have a maid service to come in regularly to keep my own home in order. The only time I actually mop and vacuum is when I am naked, under command from my superior.

"I think," she says, "I will have you finish those stairs, and then I have other plans for you. The top floor can wait for another day."

"Thank you, Mistress," I reply again. Although the house is comfortably air conditioned, I am sweaty and tired from the work. I look forward to finishing the stairs, but not only because it means my task will be over. No, it also means that Mistress Lyla has something else in store.

I finish the top stair with a silent sigh of relief, and take the bucket and sponge back to the closet under Mistress Lyla's watchful eye. Once they are put away, I return to her, kneeling in front of her on the hardwood floor of the hallway. My knees are bruised from the cleaning, but I don't even feel the discomfort. All I know is that I am at the feet of the woman I love.

"You will remember," Mistress Lyla says, "that there were quite a few things in that bag we brought from Toronto."

I say nothing, looking at the floor. How well I did remember the difficulty I had picking it up from the rug with my teeth, and how heavy it was, heavy enough that it slipped out of my mouth again. But so far I had only seen her chain and leather outfit, and the collar, leash, and paddle that were used on me in the hotel room. The bag obviously contained much more than that.

"I bought a lot of merchandise there," she continues. "Of course I am eager to try it all out, but I still don't seem to have the feel for spontaneous punishment for no reason at all. I am sure that will come in time. For now, I am satisfied to discipline you whenever I feel you have done something to deserve it."

"Mistress," I say, "surely you aren't dissatisfied with my housework. I did everything you told me to, Mistress!"

She glares at me for my sudden outburst, and I can see that she is thinking about slapping me, but then she stands back, calmly, cooly. This hauteur terrifies me and I tremble.

"You were supposed to tidy the living room," she says. "If you will come with me, I will show you where my dissatisfaction lies."

Obediently, I follow a few steps behind her. My mind races, trying to remember what I did wrong. I straightened everything up, dusted every knickknack, washed the floors, and vacuumed the carpets. What could be wrong?

Mistress Lyla points to the pile of books and papers, the one with the domination novel on top. It is unruly, scattered about. "I would hardly call that tidy," she says.

I am almost in tears. "Mistress, please!" I cry. "I

did tidy that pile, I did! I straightened everything up..." I stop suddenly, for something has clicked for me. Of course! It is yet another scene from the novel on top, and it tumbles through my mind: the submissive doing everything correctly, the dominatrix messing it up in order to punish her. I am silent. I am trapped, and no words will get me out of this.

"I believe," she says, "that you are saying I am wrong."

"Oh, no, Mistress! I'm not saying that at all!" I fall to my knees in front of her. I have lost, and my only hope is acquiescence. "You are correct, I neglected to tidy that pile. I am terribly sorry."

"Sorry," she says, "is not enough." Up until now the scene has proceeded almost as it did in the book, but at that moment Mistress Lyla takes over. My scalp is on fire, and I scream. She has grabbed a handful of my long hair and is dragging me by it.

I can only scramble on my hands and knees to try and keep up with her. She is very strong and I have no doubt that she can pull me around the entire house in this manner. When she heads for the stairs I shriek. She walks up them, her hands still in my hair, and I try my best to follow her. The stairs bang hard against my body. Half crawling, half dragged, I finally find myself at the top of that upper hallway.

Still I am pulled, right to the bedroom at the far end of the house. Here I am thrown violently to the carpet, and I can only gasp and sob. She casually discards a clump of my hair from her hand, and tears roll down my cheeks.

"Over the chair," she says, and miserably I throw myself stomach-first on it, so that my back is exposed. Then I watch as she reaches into a top drawer.

The item she pulls out is a scourge, and my eyes widen in terror. It is only a small whip, less than two feet long, but it has a thick handle that tapers down to a cruelly braided leather end.

"Now," she whispers, "I will discover the joy of making a slave scream!"

She brings it down on my back and I gasp. It is as if white-hot coals have been dropped on my flesh. She brings her arm up again and again, and the scourge licks fire across my back.

Four times it falls across my spine, and then she says, "Turn over!" I do and the chair presses hard against the welts the whip has raised. I whimper miserably.

Her target now is my upper thighs, and this is far worse. I struggle to hold my shoulders up, for relaxing them would mean bending my spine painfully to the contour of the chair. Now I can see the whip as it rises up. Mistress Lyla's expression is surprisingly calm, but in her eyes I can see the sexual excitement that I know so well. I realize that under those brightly colored pajamas is a burning, wet, needy pussy.

My legs hurt even before the whip comes down, and my eyes follow its swift curve. Five times it strikes me. Now I can feel slithering heat, and I see that it has drawn thin lines of blood across my thighs. They are horribly red against my pale skin.

The sixth and seventh lashes crisscross these red lines and I cry. With her eighth strike she gets her wish. I can control myself no longer and I scream my agony. Her cruel smile beams.

"It is everything they said," she says contentedly, and now the sexual excitement is evident. Still holding the whip, she comes to straddle my leg.

The blood stains her pajamas, but she doesn't care. I hold my arms backwards against the floor, trembling with the strain to keep my shoulders up.

She rubs hard against my flogged skin and I scream with this new agony. I can feel the heat of her cunt right through the silk as she grinds her pussy on my leg. She rides me like a horse, back and forth on my battered flesh with that needy slit.

She thrusts the handle of that whip into my face. "Suck it!" she orders, and I do. The leather is hot, sweaty, musty. I lick it and suck it deep into my mouth. Her crazed movement on my leg thrusts it hard against my tongue and I gag. This excites her even more.

Now her free hand is pinching my nipple, but I hardly feel this new torment. My leg burns and my mouth is filled with the leather device. Her hair swings wildly against my chest as she fucks my leg and my own cunt is throbbing.

When she comes, it is as explosive as ever. She all but screams with the orgasm as it rips through her and she rides my leg until every tremor is finished. Then she gets up, takes the whip from my mouth, and leaves me there. I am starved for air and I gasp, trying to catch my breath.

"Adequate," she says. "Now get up, I don't want you dripping blood on the floor. You'll lick it up if you do."

It is almost impossible to rise, but I get up, all of my body shaking. I look down at my leg; it is smeared with blood and with the pussyjuice that soaked through her silk pajamas. The rusty taste of blood is in my mouth and every muscle in my body aches. But I am thrilled. "Thank you, Mistress," I whisper.

She is busy taking off her pajamas, and I marvel again at her beautiful body. "Put these in to soak, before they are permanently stained," she orders, and I rush to comply.

When I come back she has changed into a loose-fitting robe. She looks wonderful, and I am ashamed by my appearance. It obviously annoys her also, for she says, "You are a mess."

"I am sorry, Mistress," I say.

"Well, come and clean up," she says, and I follow her. We go right down to the first floor where there is a bathroom used mostly by guests. I know that her own private, ensuite bath will never be open to me again, unless it is for me to clean. A slave's soil can never contaminate a Mistress's private chamber.

She starts the shower and orders me inside. The water is icy cold, and I hesitate. She slaps me hard on the thigh, the one that she rode so furiously, and I cry out with the pain. "Inside," she orders.

No matter how hot the weather, I enjoy my showers very warm and this is agony. Still, I have been ordered inside and that is enough for me to comply. I wash my hair and soap myself. The water causes the welts to ooze blood, which runs down my leg. Finally the bleeding stops, and I assess the damage. My leg is crisscrossed with cruel red welts. I know they will disappear in time, but it will be most painful for me until they do.

Mistress Lyla has a special salve for this, and once I have dried off—using a small, thin towel, not the luxurious thick bath sheet that I spy hanging on the wall and covet so much—she sits me down and holds the jar out to me. The medicine is thick, brown, and smells hideously like turpentine. It burns like a mineral spirit too, and I moan and try to concentrate on something else to keep my nausea at bay. This obviously delights Mistress Lyla, and she takes the jar from me and slathers the ointment on the stripes she has laid across my back. They burn just as horribly and I know that the flogging must have drawn blood there too.

"Now come with me," she says, and stiffly I follow her. The stripes on my leg burn fresh with each movement. She takes me back upstairs to the bedroom where I received the punishment. I look at the chair and marvel at the Mistress that Lyla Kirk has become.

"Stand there," she orders, pointing to a spot beside another chair, and I do so. Now she comes back with another item, a leather harness, but with something on it that I can't immediately identify.

She holds it up to show me, and I am struck by the originality of it. It is a paging device, the kind used to reach executives on the run. During the trade shows I wear them almost constantly.

Mistress Lyla indicates that I should hold out my hand, and she lays it in my palm while pushing a button on the side of it. It vibrates hard; it is a silent pager.

The harness it is attached to is a leather device, most commonly used to hold dildos when women fuck other women. The pager is attached to the leather piece where the plastic penis usually goes.

Now she sits on the chair and this harness is fitted to my waist, and I understand why the clerk measured me so carefully. The straps fit perfectly and when the buckle is tightened, the pager just rubs up against the top of my clit. I understand completely. The small plastic box will be hidden by a skirt and if I sit carefully it will not interfere with my normal activities.

"You are going to leave now," Mistress Lyla says.

"I will call you on the telephone and actually speak to you when I want you. This pager is not an indication that you are to call me."

As she adjusts the leather straps one more time, it all makes sense to me. This pager, which vibrates so strongly, just touches that most sensitive place in my slit.

"You will wear this until I tell you otherwise," she continues. "You will take it off to wash and whenever you need to use the toilet, but once you are finished you will put it right back on, in exactly the same way I have adjusted it here. Do you understand?"

"Yes, Mistress," I say.

"Then dress and leave," she says simply. It is difficult to walk down the long staircase with my injured leg and my stiff back, but much easier than the way I went up the first time, my Mistress's hands in my hair. I collect my dress in the hallway and slip it over my head. Fortunately the skirt falls below my knee and covers the horrible marks left by the flogging.

Mistress Lyla stands at the top of the staircase, and I turn before I leave. "Jennifer," she says, "I will say that you did an excellent job of cleaning the house."

"Thank you, Mistress!" I sigh, and I long to be able to run up the stairs and kneel before her. I love her so! But permission to do so is not given, and I am under orders to leave. When I swing the front door open, the outside heat is like a blast furnace.

"Jennifer?" I turn in the open door. "Yes, Mistress?" She smiles at me. "I understand it now," she says. Then she turns and walks away from me, down the hall, to the bedroom. I can't control my smile.

The men working on the garage stop to watch me as I walk by. It is difficult and I put everything into walking as normally as possible, even though my body screams with agony. I pray that my wounds will not open again and stain my leg crimson. Eventually they lose interest and go back to their work, all of which is taking place inside the former slaves' quarters.

The straps of my harness rub on my skin, which is already sweaty from the heat, and I know that they will eventually make marks of their own. The pager is smooth and hard against my clit. I wonder how long it will be before she calls. I wonder just how I will be able to wait.

"PHOTO SESSION"
(from *Romantic Encounters*)

"**Y**ou're late," Andrea admonished.

"Sorry," Julie said, trying to grab her coat, her bag, and the car door all at the same time. "I got tied up."

"Figuratively or literally?"

"Just in a manner of speaking, unfortunately," Julie smiled. Andrea put the car into gear as her friend fastened her seat belt.

"It wasn't your virgin, was it?"

"I only wish! No, it's still a little too early for that. But she did find out I'm a lesbian, though."

"That's a start," Andrea said. "How did she take it?"

"Better than I thought she would," Julie said. "Now I'm determined she's mine. Don't worry, dear," she teased, as she noticed Andrea's longing expression, "I'll tell you all about it."

They pulled up in front of an old warehouse; lights in the upstairs windows announced that the loft was used for more than storage. Much of it was a photographer's studio, and there was much work waiting for them upstairs.

The two hung their coats on a rack by the door and walked inside, assessing the situation. Immediately they liked what they saw.

Four women were working in a corner of the huge studio. One was setting up lights and adjusting a camera tripod. Another was making notes on a clipboard while two of the women, completely naked, were looking through a rack of clothes. Some of the items hanging from it were made of leather, some silk and lace, and, at one end, several nasty devices gleamed in the bright lights.

"Sorry we're late, Madison," Andrea said as she walked over.

"We certainly wouldn't start without you, Andrea," Madison said, as she put her clipboard down and ran her fingers through her long blonde hair. She was fully dressed, as was Lucy, the gorgeous black woman who was checking her light meter; but Julie noted that they both wore clothes that could be slipped away easily, and she felt her pussy twitch at the thought.

"So who do we have here?" Julie asked.

"Andrea, Julie, I'd like to introduce Carla and Lorna," Madison said. Hearing their names, the two women came over and shook hands with Julie and Andrea. They seemed completely unconcerned that they were stark naked.

"I hope you don't mind if I look at you," Julie said, very businesslike, for she knew just the effect she was looking for, and wanted to make sure that she would achieve it here tonight.

"Not at all," Carla said, and the two women stood with a polished ease that showed off their professional training as models.

Julie and Andrea walked all around them, looking carefully. Madison had done her job well; they were magnificent. Both were tall and willowy, their bodies perfectly proportioned and enticing. Lorna's dark skin shone under the hot lights and Julie admired the way the shadows played under her firm, well-shaped breasts. Her pubic hair was jet black and tightly curled on her mound; through her slightly parted thighs, Julie could see that her pussylips had been shaved clean. From behind, her ass was tight. Julie had to keep herself from reaching out to grab one perfect cheek in each hand.

Carla's skin was pale, a fine contrast to Lorna. Her tits were a bit bigger, with huge nipples; the right nipple was pierced and decorated with a small gold ring that Julie longed to touch. Her strawberry blonde pussyhair matched the curls that came to the nape of her neck. Julie could imagine placing a kiss right there, where the hair ended. Her legs were impossibly long and delicately shaped; Andrea could see them spread wide apart, trembling, as her cunt was sucked.

"You'll do just fine," Julie finally said, and the two women smiled. They knew what was involved with this particular job, and they had been looking forward to it for a long time; and being approved by a top editor and a powerful publisher just made it even sweeter.

They also liked the props that had been set up in the studio. There was a large bed with spotless white sheets, a soft, overstuffed chaise lounge, and a wing chair, upholstered in black velvet. On the other side were items completely at odds with the conventional props. Here was a gymnast's horse, made of firm tan leather with wooden handles; a hard, straight-backed wooden chair with cuffs screwed to the arms and legs; and a very unusual prop for photography: an aluminum stepladder, open into the familiar triangle.

"A stepladder?" Andrea asked.

"I was in the hardware store the other day, and they had a whole display of ladders in the front window," Madison said. "Some big sale or something. Anyway, I saw this and immediately thought of all the possibilities, so I bought it."

"You're a genius, Madison," Julie said as she started to run in her mind all the ways that a woman could be posed on it. "Someday I swear you're going to find a way to make an eggbeater seem erotic."

"Speaking of erotic," the blonde woman said, "I have your latest release, hot off the press. Let me get it."

She went over to a small box and came back with two copies of an oversized paperback, which Julie and Andrea hurried to see. Flipping through the pages, they were pleased with what they saw.

This was the other side of Coats Publishing. It was the latest book from Sapphic Press, a subsidiary of the larger company, and a pet project of the two women. The romance novels had made Coats a household word, but when Andrea and Julie wanted something to read, they turned to their own Sapphic Press for books more to their liking.

The company had been in business for ten years. In that time it had turned out several hundred titles. Most of them were regular paperbacks, but recently they had been producing oversized books, containing photographs such as the ones they were going to take that night. As successful as the smaller novels had been, the large illustrated volumes were outselling them rapidly, much to the delight of the company owner and editor.

This particular volume was dedicated to a number of pleasures, and the models and photographer cooled their heels and waited while Andrea and Julie looked through their copies. "The photographs reproduced extremely well," Andrea said, and Madison had to agree.

"I like this one," Julie said, and Andrea looked over to see the page opened to a hot shot of two women kissing, their lips just a fraction of an inch apart, so that their tongues were visible, touching each other. "I forgot we included that one; I'm glad we did."

"How about this one?" Andrea asked. She had turned to a shot of the same two models, one bound tightly with nylon cord so that her tits were squeezed out almost obscenely, the other standing over her with thigh-high boots and a riding crop in one hand which she was using to caress one taut, swollen nipple.

"I almost came when I saw that one," Madison said, and the two models looked up appreciatively, hoping that they would be able to elicit a similar response from this gorgeous, classy lady who had selected them for this particular evening. They became even more interested when Andrea reached out, almost unconsciously, and, without taking her eyes from the book, began to rub the back of Madison's neck. Madison arched her back, thoroughly enjoying the touch.

"Well, we're not getting anything done by standing here reading," Julie finally said, as she put the book down. "I can look at that later. Why check out pictures when we have the real thing?"

That put everyone into action. Madison went over to the rack to select clothes, Carla and Lorna following behind, still deliciously naked; Lucy turned on lights and adjusted the diffusing umbrellas; and Andrea and Julie sat down in the comfortable chairs that had been provided for them, facing the large bed.

There was no need for a screen for the models to change behind, and Andrea and Julie were treated to the sight of them putting on the outfits that Madison selected. Once that was done, they were paraded by the publisher and editor for final approval.

It was given. Carla's fair skin was set off by a dark blue silk robe, while Lorna was dressed in white satin pajamas that covered her completely. Now it was over to the bed, where Lorna stretched out. Madison adjusted the lapels and the trouser legs of the pajamas as Lucy got the camera ready to shoot.

"Now," Julie said, "I want to take this in a sequence almost like you would for a 'girlie' magazine. Lorna's supposed to be asleep"—the camera started to click—"and that's when Carla comes in and finds her."

The two women were professionals and Julie was impressed by how smoothly they moved into their positions. Lorna positioned herself on the bed to show off her beautiful body to its best advantage, the curves of her delicious breasts sheathed in white satin.

Her thighs were parted, one knee bent, and Julie found herself wanting that crotch, which was inviting even though it was fully clothed. Julie had to squirm on her chair and she shivered as she ground her throbbing cunt into the seat. Andrea turned and smiled at her, and Julie knew that she was just as excited.

Carla now came over by the bed. The blue robe was slightly open, and Julie could catch a glimpse of a nipple with its gold accent and the hint of curly strawberry blonde hair between the thighs. She pushed again hard against her seat. Even though she had seen both women completely naked only moments before, their positions and the deftly placed clothes made it feel as if she was only seeing them for the first time. These women were good! This book was going to sell!

Lucy had the camera ready and as she and Madison set up the shots, the shutter clicked over and over, catching it all. The action was a combination of movement and then posing, moving and posing, as the camera caught them in the act of discovery. The film made its way through the camera, capturing Carla unbuttoning Lorna's white satin pajama top and applying her tongue to the huge chocolate-colored nipples that Julie found her mouth watering for.

"Hold like that, please," Lucy said, and Andrea's hand strayed down to her thigh as she watched Carla pause, her tongue on Lorna's nipple. Then she looked at the camera as she slowly lapped all around it, making sure that Lucy caught her pink tongue circling all around the hard nub before taking it into her mouth.

Lorna was now lying with the pajama top flung

open, her body covered only by the satin trousers. Carla took her time sliding these smoothly off Lorna's long, dark legs, and following the fabric with her tongue. "Beautiful!" Lucy said, and she moved in close with a smaller, hand-held camera to get the sight of Lorna's skin glistening with the trail of saliva and Carla's tongue caressing the flawless skin. Julie could see through Lucy's thin white shirt; her own nipples were as hard as Lorna's as she moved in close with the camera to catch every moment.

The shutter continued to click as Lucy now focused on the blonde pussy, visible through the open robe. "Touch her there," she said, and Lorna reached up and caressed Carla's thighs. Her fingers were dark and rich against Carla's pale skin. Carla couldn't help moaning when Lorna finally touched her pussy, and Lucy came in close to get a shot of Lorna's fingers shiny with cuntjuice.

"That's so nice," Andrea whispered, and Julie turned to see that her friend had a hand inside of her skirt, kneading her own breast. That was what Julie loved most about these photo sessions; Madison made sure that the models were always cool about whatever direction the proceedings might take, and Julie, Andrea, Lucy and Madison had been doing them long enough to know that if they didn't turn into fuckfests, there was definitely something wrong.

"Now lick her, please," Madison said, and at that moment, the professional models were no longer just working at their jobs. Julie was pleased to see that with the first touch of Carla's tongue on Lorna's swollen pussy, they were now passionate lovers who just happened to have someone snapping pictures of them. It would mean that instead of staged shots, their next book would feature some hot photos that would definitely increase sales.

It also meant a far more interesting photo shoot for the onlookers, and Julie's hand was on her own breast shortly. The nipple was hard and she tweaked it, and when Andrea noticed what she was doing, she reached over to give some attention to the other one.

"A little more to the side, please," Lucy said, and Carla moved slightly to give a better view of her tongue deep in Lorna's cunt. She used it to push the thick lips aside, and Lucy let out a sigh as Carla sucked hard and pulled Lorna's pussylips out with her mouth. Lorna was moaning, her head thrown back.

Carla dropped the robe now and Lucy moved around to get a shot of her sopping pussy from behind. Her asscheeks were tight and luscious, and her tight cunthair shone with juice. She fingered herself as she licked Lorna's cunt and she couldn't help rocking her hips back and forth as she did, giving Lucy a prime opportunity to capture it on film. Fortunately, Lucy was using a tripod for this, for she was rubbing her own cunt through her jeans with her free hand and moaning softly as she did.

"Now can we get you on the lounge?" Madison asked. Lorna and Carla were both reluctant to stop, but they did, and at Madison's direction, Carla laid out on the sofa, her head between the arms, her legs spread out on the open part of the couch. Now it was Lorna's turn to taste pussy, and Julie and Andrea responded to this treat by putting their hands between each other's legs. Andrea was wearing a skirt, and Julie found that, as was her custom, she was wearing nothing under it. Julie rubbed her fingers together so that the hot fluid spread all over her hand.

Julie was wearing satin underpants, and Andrea rubbed the smooth, warm fabric right against Julie's throbbing cunt. Their chairs were facing each other and they kissed, long and hard, but broke away finally to turn their attention back to the two women who were making love to both the camera and each other.

Lorna turned slowly and moved up on the lounge to put herself over Carla, but she never left the sex-sodden pussy she was eating so eagerly. Carla reached up to grab dark asscheeks and pull Lorna's shaved slit down to her mouth. Lucy was moving like crazy now, focusing and shooting with the camera on the tripod. When something really struck her fancy she moved in close with a hand-held camera to catch every wet lick and pussy-filled mouth.

When Julie turned to look at Andrea, she saw her friend removing her blouse. "That's longer than you usually last," she grinned.

"I always tell myself I'm going to hold off a bit longer," Andrea said. "Willpower. But then, the sluts that Madison gets are always so hot, and I just can't stop myself. Julie, suck my tits, will you? Please!"

The pleading was unnecessary. In a moment, Julie was bent over and on the huge chocolate nipples. Andrea groaned loudly, and for a moment, the two models on the lounge looked up. They were momentarily surprised; they had been told that this might happen, but it was still unexpected to look up and see what they did. When Andrea moaned again, and Julie put her hand under her own skirt to push her satin panties into her crotch, the models smiled and then went back to what they were doing.

The air was now filled with moans and the rich smell of female flesh. Madison's shirt was unbuttoned;

when she was working the stationary camera, Lucy would put one hand up under her baggy sweatshirt to fondle one of her own nipples. When Madison came up from behind her, reached under and grabbed them herself, the photographer took a step backward and reveled in the feeling of Madison's hard, naked tits pressing against her back.

The women on the lounge were very close to coming; it was evident from their writhing and the loud moans they made even as they pushed their tongues hard into each other's cunts. Lorna had two fingers in Carla's pussy, and she was fucking hard and fast with them; Lucy kept pressing the shutter cable, taking picture after picture of the action. When Carla came, it was so hard that she screamed. Julie sucked hard on Andrea's tits as they both enjoyed the sound.

Madison called a halt to the action, then came over to the lounge with an item which she gave to Carla. "As we discussed," she said, and then stepped out of camera range. She winked at Julie and Andrea, who were eagerly watching to see what it was she had given them.

It turned out to be a dildo, but a very interesting one. There were actually two cocks on it: one very large and long, the other somewhat smaller and shorter, placed just below the first. It was very pale pink, to show off best against Lorna's dark skin.

"Madison, that's amazing!" Andrea said. "Where did you ever find that?"

The blonde woman smiled and winked. "My bedroom closet." Julie asked if she could come over and look through it for other delightful treasures sometime.

The women changed positions on the lounge, with

the darker woman now stretched out and Carla sitting on the floor in front of her. Lorna was so wet that there was no need for lubrication. Carla slowly rubbed the head of the larger cock up and down the full length of Lorna's ruby slit, parting the lips with it and tickling the hard button of her clit. Then she did the same with the smaller one, until both the heads were shiny with hot juice. When she put first one cock and then the other into her mouth to suck off the wine-rich fluid, Lucy snapped picture after picture.

Once again she wet the two heads with cuntjuice, and then positioned the larger head against the entrance to Lorna's hot hole. She pushed it in so slowly that Lorna begged her to hurry, but she wanted this to last. When the large dildo was halfway in, the smaller cock was positioned right at the entry to Lorna's tightly whorled anus.

"Push it in!" Madison whispered, and everyone else watching nodded. Lorna herself was begging for both holes to be filled.

Carla made them wait until everyone watching was so horny that there wasn't a pussy without a hand rubbing it slowly. She bent down and licked all around Lorna's cuntlips, kissing where the rubber dildo sank into hot flesh. She flashed her tongue a few times over Lorna's clit until her lover was so hot that she tried to push the double dildo in herself. Then, ever so slowly, she began to penetrate that forbidden opening.

Lucy was so transfixed by the whole scene that Madison had to remind her to take pictures, which she did; photo after photo, until it seemed that the shutter never closed.

It took forever until the solid handle end of the

dildo was tight against Lorna's body, and everyone in the room let out a sigh when it was finally there. Lorna was breathless, reveling in the full feeling of having both holes jammed with the soft pink latex. Then she pleaded to be fucked.

Carla did. She worked slowly at first, in and out, and both rubber cocks gleamed wet with juice. Then faster and faster, until finally both dildos were ramming in full force, and Lorna was moaning and gasping with the pleasure that it gave her.

When she came, both cocks in as far as they would go, she trembled violently and cried out. Lucy came in close and caught a shot of her ruby pussy filled with plastic cock and so much sweet juice that it ran down her thighs.

"Take a break," Madison said, almost unnecessarily; for Lorna and Carla were now beside each other, breathing hard, Lorna trying to gain her composure following her massive orgasm.

At that moment, Madison realized that Andrea was behind her. She stood up straight as she felt the publisher's hands reach around her to hold one perfect breast in each palm.

In a moment, both of them were undressed. All eyes turned to watch them. Their kiss was long and unhurried—they had all night!—but stunningly passionate nevertheless. When they parted, Andrea took Madison's hand and led her over to the black velvet wing chair.

The blonde woman looked perfect within the confines of its wings. The highly polished wooden floor was hard, but Andrea was content to get on her knees so that she could be close to Madison's pussy. It took only a moment for her to spread the shapely legs

222 I THE BEST OF LINDSAY WELSH

and expose the blonde pussy that she desired. Then her tongue was deep inside, and Madison moaned and put her hands to her nipples to pull and twist at them.

Lucy watched for a little while, and then could stand it no longer. She threw off the baggy sweatshirt and her jeans and walked over to the chair. Andrea groaned as Lucy slipped under her to take one perfect nipple into her mouth and suck hard on it. Then Lucy pushed Andrea's knees apart, laid on her back on the hard floor, and started to lap at the pussy that was right over her mouth.

Lorna and Carla watched with interest. Both of them were relaxed, but started to get excited again at the sight. But it was Julie who was consumed with it, and her hand was under her skirt and rubbing her cunt as hard and fast as she could.

The scene would inflame anyone. The luscious blonde woman, fondling her own tits, sitting in the chair with her legs open and her pussy being eaten out by another woman who had a woman under her, lapping at *her* cunt! Lucy's hand was between her legs, fingering her clit, and all three of them were moaning as their pussies were worked over.

"Get over here," Julie said. Carla was over in a moment, kneeling on the floor in front of her. Julie lifted up her skirt but left on her panties, and Julie sighed as she felt the heat of Carla's tongue on her pussy right through the satin. Carla sucked in, running cloth and hot female flesh over her lips, and Julie moaned. She looked over to see that Lorna was watching them intently, her hand between her legs.

The whole studio was hot with sex. The photographer's lights, still on, lit up the three women as they ate each other out, and showed up Lorna as she whipped her fingers over her clit and pushed the fingers of her other hand deep inside her hole.

Andrea was in heaven. She stopped for a moment to admire the rich, flowery pussy that she had been licking, now deliciously wet with saliva and smeared with the steamy juice that had come out of Madison's creamy vagina. She pulled the soft lips apart and admired the folds and the hard clit inside, while Madison pushed her hips forward and begged to be touched some more. Andrea, meanwhile, was rocking her own hips slowly back and forth over Lucy's tongue and reveling in the warmth that went right through her entire body from the mouth on her cunt.

Andrea used the tip of her finger to excite Madison's clit until it was rockhard and trembling. Then, her finger still on it, she moved her thumb to the opening of Madison's needy vagina. It was so well lubricated that she slipped inside effortlessly, and Madison groaned as she was penetrated. Andrea expertly moved her whole hand back and forth, alternating, so that Madison's clit was teased as Andrea's thumb pulled out of her; and then, when her whole body was taut and waiting, she was filled again. The rhythm was like being fucked and licked at the same time, and in no time at all, the blonde woman was groaning and thrashing on the chair, her whole body trembling as she came.

Only a moment later, Lucy brought herself to climax with her hand, her tongue still on Andrea's pussy. Andrea, not to be left out, was grinding down on her now, so that very shortly she joined her two lovers in a shattering peak that left her gasping for breath as she knelt on the floor.

Julie was still getting her pussy licked, but when she saw the three women come, she motioned for

Lorna to get up. They kissed deeply, Julie thoroughly enjoying the taste of her own cunt given back to her on the tongue of another woman. Her fingers played with the small gold nipple ring that she had so coveted; she loved the way she could pull the nipple out with it and liked its warmth between her fingers. She wanted desperately to come, but now she wanted to wait and stretch out the longing even more, because she had an idea of what was yet to transpire in the studio. She was patient. She knew that when she did come, it was going to take her apart.

Julie was still the only one in the studio still dressed, however, and while the others got up slowly and traded kisses and soft caresses, she removed her clothes carefully and left them in a neat pile in the floor, pretending not to notice the appreciative looks that she got as Lorna and Carla were treated to the sight of her well-kept body and luscious breasts unclothed for the first time.

Madison was setting up the second set of shots while Lucy reloaded the cameras and moved the lights around. Now they were focused on the other side of the room, where the horse, the hideous cuffed chair, and the aluminum stepladder were placed. The sexual tension was running high even now, even after all of the orgasms, as the lights and shadows turned these otherwise-harmless items into sinister props.

The costumes were handed out and the two women dressed quickly. Lorna was given a black leather corset that pushed her tits up over the top of the bra and exposed her hard nipples; her pussy was uncovered, but the leather garters attached to the corset held up black fishnet stockings. Her feet were thrust into high black polished-leather boots; her hands were covered with buttery leather gloves that reached almost to her elbows.

Carla's costume was much simpler: a leather collar about her throat and black leather cuffs that buckled around her wrists with shiny silver buckles. Identical cuffs went around her ankles, buckled tight against her pale skin.

The final touch was a very long, very thin gold chain, which Madison attached to the ring in Carla's nipple. It would make a most attractive leash.

The first shots were done on the horse. Julie's tastes generally ran more to romance than to dominance, but occasionally she enjoyed rough trade, and tonight she was in the mood to see it. The fact that her readers would buy such books in droves was pleasurable as well, but right now, when everything was happening right in front of her, it was her own private show and she was ready and waiting for it.

Lucy and Madison set up shot after shot. They had Carla straddle the horse, her wrist cuffs joined with a small length of chrome chain that was looped between the wooden handles, and later on a snap ring was used to hold her ankles around the bottom of it. With her ass presented so enticingly, Lorna's leather-clad palm smacked down several times on the pale cheeks until they glowed red with the spanking. Lucy's camera caught not only the disciplined flesh, but also the wetness of her pussy from the blows.

"I like that; give her a few more," Andrea said, and Julie looked over at her friend, completely naked, her eyes wide, one hand on her crotch, another on her nipple. Lorna responded by smacking the tops of Carla's thighs. Soon the sensitive skin was as ripe and red as the battered globes of her asscheeks.

Lucy finished up with her photos here, and then the two were moved to the wooden chair. Now Carla was pushed into the chair—as before, they got into their roles completely, and Julie's excitement grew when she saw Lorna shove her captive backward as a dominatrix would, while Carla dropped her head and gave herself over to the stronger woman dressed in leather. The heavy cuffs were removed from Carla's wrists and ankles and were replaced by the restraints on the chair. A chain was snapped to the ring on her collar, which was wrapped around one of the rungs on the back of the chair, holding her upright against it.

Madison was thoroughly enjoying herself as she positioned her models, and Julie could see drops of fluid on her blonde pussyhair. She had Lorna pull on the gold chain, so that Carla's nipple was stretched out, and one high-heeled boot was carefully placed between Carla's shackled legs so that the stiletto heel tip slipped in between the thick, wet pussylips. Lucy spent almost a whole roll of film there, trying to get every angle of the razor-thin leather heel shiny with cuntjuice and wrapped in pubic hair.

"Now lick her," Madison said, and Lorna lifted one shapely leg to rest on the back of the chair. Her dark pussy was near Carla's face, and the bound woman applied her tongue eagerly. Her sighs at being allowed this treat were mixed with groans as Lorna pulled hard on the gold-chain leash attached to the sensitive pierced nipple. More shots were taken as Lorna moved back and Carla strained against the chain that held her by the throat to the back of the chair in an attempt to reach the treat that had been taken away from her.

Finally the shot was finished, and Carla was released

from the hard wooden chair. The leather restraints were cuffed back on her hands and legs, and long chrome chains were snapped on to join them together. Now it was over to the aluminum stepladder. By the looks on the faces of the models, Carla was nervous and Lorna was thrilled at what was about to transpire.

The chains clanked against the metal ladder as Carla was ordered to climb it. Once on top, she was forced to straddle it, and Julie couldn't help wincing when the shackled woman sat down on the top step, for the ladder had been kept out of the lights up until now and the aluminum was ice cold. Carla's discomfort was compounded by the difficult position, for she had one leg on either side of the ladder's legs and she was spread as far as she could possibly be within the confines of the heavy chains that held her feet together.

Lorna was now handed a black leather riding crop and told to use her imagination. It was obviously very vivid, for she ran the crop through her fingers several times, slowly—Carla's eyes never left it—and then put it to use.

Her captive had to kiss it, and then it was thrust between her lips so that she fellated its musty leather handle. When the crop was shiny wet with saliva, Lorna then moved it farther down, and very slowly, the camera clicking all the while, pushed it deep into the hot recesses of Carla's cunt. Once it was in, she was fucked with it, slowly at first, then faster, until the women watching were fucking themselves as well with their hands.

"Have you got enough pictures?" Julie asked. She was fingering her own clit, and she wanted desperately to come.

"I think I do," Lucy answered.

"Then," Julie said, as she got up from her seat and went to get her bag, "I can't wait. This little slut belongs to me."

The hot lights were switched off. The photo session over, Andrea, Madison, and Lucy waited eagerly, knowing what was coming. The two models stood uncertainly. They knew something was up, but of course they had no idea.

"Get her off there," Andrea said, and Lucy moved to unsnap the chains from Carla's cuffs. The dark leather, so attractive against her pale skin, was left on, as was the gold chain attached to the nipple ring. Carla was taken off the ladder and told to stand at the edge of the bed.

Julie returned, and all of the women, Carla and Lorna included, looked on admiringly. She wore a leather harness about her hips. Attached to it was a huge rubber cock, shiny with her own juice from having been rubbed across her soaking cunt.

She stood behind Carla and rocked her hips so that the cock slid in between her thighs. Carla moaned; the rubber dildo felt arousing against her pussy. Then Julie pushed her forward, so that her hands were on the mattress, her ass presented for Julie's pleasure.

Julie put the head of the cock against Carla's cunt and slid it in smoothly. "I'm going to fuck you," she whispered, and as Carla sighed with the fullness in her vagina, Julie thrust the cock in again and again.

"Please fuck me!" Carla couldn't control herself; it felt so good to have Julie's prick in her. "Fuck me, fill me!" Julie did, ramming the cock in.

Julie then groaned herself as Andrea came up behind her and reached for her clit. Sandwiched in between the two women, Julie gasped for breath, moaning, as she fucked one woman and had her throbbing clit massaged from behind by another.

She had the gold nipple-ring chain in one hand, pulling on it, while she held Carla's hips and pulled her towards her as she jammed the cock home. Each thrust ground her clit across Andrea's hand and brought her even closer to the climax she craved.

When she felt the buildup start to crack and release, she squeezed the balls of the rubber cock hard. A jet of warm water shot out of the head and splashed into Carla's cunt. Hot from being inside there, it spilled out of her and poured down both their legs. At the same time, Julie cried out as Andrea's hand brought her off, hard and trembling.

Julie sat on the bed; she had come so intensely that she was weak. Madison came over and licked the rubber cock dry, savoring the female juice on it before running her tongue further down to lick the nectar from Julie's cunt.

Andrea grinned at her friend, who was gasping, trying to catch her breath. "I trust you're not going to break your little virgin in like that, are you?" she smiled.

It was some time before Julie could even reply. "I have to do this," she said. "If I blow off like this, it'll keep me from grabbing her and taking her all at once."

"Good idea," Andrea said as she caressed Julie's taut nipples with a fingertip. "There will be plenty of time for this once you get her going."

"If I do," Julie said. "I've still got to get her interested in me, you know. Don't forget that."

"Lick me! Julie, please lick me there!" Linda gasped as her hips lifted off the bed, trying to grind her pussy right into the buzzing vibrator. She had a magazine open in front of her, to a picture of two women eating each other out, but her eyes were closed tightly. In her mind's eye, she was the woman on top; the luscious body under her belonged to none other than Julie Gray.

"Eat me, Julie! Lick my cunt, make me come!" Linda could all but taste Julie's pussy, feel her hot tongue on her own clit, smell her female perfume. The vibrator had her close—so close—and now she was slipping over the edge, moaning as loud as she could, trembling while her pussy surged against the dildo.

After a long time, Linda turned it off and kissed it. "Thank you, thank you, Julie," she whispered to the woman she wanted, the woman whose pussy she longed to lick and whose lips she dreamed of kissing. Now, she thought to herself, if only she could get Julie Gray interested in her. If only. Oh, if only.

The Masquerade
Erotic Newsletter

◆ ◆

FICTION, ESSAYS, REVIEWS, PHOTOGRAPHY, INTERVIEWS, EXPOSÉS, AND MUCH MORE!

"One of my favorite sex zines featuring some of the best articles on erotica, fetishes, sex clubs and the politics of porn." —*Factsheet Five*

"I recommend a subscription to *The Masquerade Erotic Newsletter*.... They feature short articles on "the scene"...an occasional fiction piece, and reviews of other erotic literature. Recent issues have featured intelligent prose by the likes of Trish Thomas, David Aaron Clark, Pat Califia, Laura Antoniou, Lily Burana, John Preston, and others.... it's good stuff." —*Black Sheets*

"A classy, bi-monthly magazine..." —*Betty Paginated*

"It's always a treat to see a copy of *The Masquerade Erotic Newsletter*, for it brings a sophisticated and unexpected point of view to bear on the world of erotica, and does this with intelligence, tolerance, and compassion." —Martin Shepard, co-publisher, The Permanent Press

"Publishes great articles, interviews and pix which in many cases are truly erotic and which deal non-judgementally with the full array of human sexuality, a far cry from much of the material which passes itself off under that title.... *Masquerade Erotic Newsletter* is fucking great." —*Eddie, the Magazine*

"We always enjoy receiving your *Masquerade Newsletter* and seeing the variety of subjects covered...." —*body art*

"*Masquerade Erotic Newsletter* is probably the best newsletter I have ever seen." —*Secret International*

"The latest issue is absolutely lovely. Marvelous images...."
—*The Boudoir Noir*

"I must say that the *Newsletter* is fabulous...."
—Tuppy Owens,
Publisher, Author, Sex Therapist

"Fascinating articles on all aspects of sex..." —*Desire*

◆ ◆

The Masquerade
Erotic Newsletter

"Here's a very provocative, very professional [newsletter]...made up of intelligent erotic writing... Stimulating, yet not sleazy photos add to the picture and also help make this zine a high quality publication." —Gray Areas

From **Masquerade Books**, the World's Leading Publisher of Erotica, comes *The Masquerade Erotic Newsletter*—the best source for provocative, cutting-edge fiction, sizzling pictorials, scintillating and illuminating exposes of the sex industry, and probing reviews of the latest books and videos.

Featured writers and articles have included:

Lars Eighner • *Why I Write Gay Erotica*
Pat Califia • *Among Us, Against Us*
Felice Picano • *An Interview with Samuel R. Delany*
Samuel R. Delany • *The Mad Man* (excerpt)
Maxim Jakubowski • *Essex House: The Rise and Fall of Speculative Erotica*
Red Jordan Arobateau • *Reflections of a Lesbian Trick*
Aaron Travis • *Lust*
Nancy Ava Miller, M. Ed. • *Beyond Personal*
Tuppy Owens • *Female Erotica in Great Britain*
Trish Thomas • *From Dyke to Dude*
Barbara Nitke • *Resurrection*
and many more....

The newsletter has also featured stunning photo essays by such masters of fetish photography as **Robert Chouraqui, Eric Kroll, Richard Kern,** and **Trevor Watson**.

A one-year subscription (6 issues) to the *Newsletter* costs $30.00. Use the accompanying coupon to subscribe now—for an uninterrupted string of the most provocative of pleasures (as well as a special gift, offered to subscribers only!).

ROSEBUD BOOKS

THE ROSEBUD READER

Rosebud Books—the hottest-selling line of lesbian erotica available—here collects the very best of the best. Rosebud has contributed greatly to the burgeoning genre of lesbian erotica—to the point that authors like Lindsay Welsh, Aarona Griffin and Valentina Cilescu are among the hottest and most closely watched names in lesbian and gay publishing. Here are the finest moments from Rosebud's contemporary classics. $5.95/319-8

LOVECHILD

GAG

From New York's thriving poetry scene comes this explosive volume of work from one of the bravest, most cutting young writers you'll ever encounter. The poems in *Gag* take on American hypocrisy with uncommon energy, and announce Lovechild as a writer of unique and unforgettable rage. $5.95/369-4

ALISON TYLER

THE BLUE ROSE

The tale of a modern sorority—fashioned after a Victorian girls' school. Ignited to the heights of passion by erotic tales of the Victorian age, a group of lusty young women are encouraged to act out their forbidden fantasies—all under the tutelage of Mistresses Emily and Justine, two avid practitioners of hard-core discipline! $5.95/335-X

ELIZABETH OLIVER

THE SM MURDER: Murder at Roman Hill

Intrepid lesbian P.I.s Leslie Patrick and Robin Penny take on a really hot case: the murder of the notorious Felicia Roman. The circumstances of the crime lead the pair on an excursion through the leatherdyke underground, where motives—and desires—run deep. But as Leslie and Robin soon find, every woman harbors her own closely guarded secret.... $5.95/353-8

PAGAN DREAMS

Cassidy and Samantha plan a vacation at a secluded bed-and-breakfast, hoping for a little personal time alone. Their hostess, however, has different plans. The lovers are plunged into a world of dungeons and pagan rites, as the merciless Anastasia steals Samantha for her own. B&B—B&D-style! $5.95/295-7

SUSAN ANDERS

PINK CHAMPAGNE

Tasty, torrid tales of butch/femme couplings—from a writer more than capable of describing the special fire ignited when opposites collide. Tough as nails or soft as silk, these women seek out their antitheses, intent on working out the details of their own personal theory of difference. $5.95/282-5

LAVENDER ROSE

Anonymous

A classic collection of lesbian literature: From the writings of Sappho, Queen of the island Lesbos, to the turn-of-the-century *Black Book of Lesbianism*; from *Tips to Maidens* to *Crimson Hairs*, a recent lesbian saga—here are the great but little-known lesbian writings and revelations. $4.95/208-6

EDITED BY LAURA ANTONIOU

LEATHERWOMEN II

A follow-up volume to the popular and controversial *Leatherwomen*. Laura Antoniou turns an editor's discerning eye to the writing of women on the edge—resulting in a collection sure to ignite libidinal flames. Leave taboos behind—because these Leatherwomen know no limits.... $4.95/229-9

ROSEBUD BOOKS

LEATHERWOMEN

These fantasies, from the pens of new or emerging authors, break every rule imposed on women's fantasies. The hottest stories from some of today's newest and most outrageous writers make this an unforgettable exploration of the female libido. $4.95/3095-4

LESLIE CAMERON

THE WHISPER OF FANS

"Just looking into her eyes, she felt that she knew a lot about this woman. She could see strength, boldness, a fresh sense of aliveness that rocked her to the core. In turn she felt open, revealed under the woman's gaze—all her secrets already told. No need of shame or artifice…." $5.95/259-0

AARONA GRIFFIN

PASSAGE AND OTHER STORIES

An S/M romance. Lovely Nina is frightened by her lesbian passions until she finds herself infatuated with a woman she spots at a local café. One night Nina follows her and finds herself enmeshed in an endless maze leading to a world where women test the edges of sexuality and power. $4.95/3057-1

VALENTINA CILESCU

THE ROSEBUD SUTRA

"Women are hardly ever known in their true light, though they may love others, or become indifferent towards them, may give them delight, or abandon them, or may extract from them all the wealth that they possess." So says *The Rosebud Sutra*—a volume promising women's inner secrets. One woman learns to use these secrets in a quest for pleasure with a succession of lady loves…. $4.95/242-6

THE HAVEN

J craves domination, and her perverse appetites lead her to the Haven: the isolated sanctuary Ros and Annie call home. Soon J forces her way into the couple's world, bringing unspeakable lust and cruelty into their lives. The Dominatrix Who Came to Dinner! $4.95/165-9

MISTRESS MINE

Sophia Cranleigh sits in prison, accused of authoring the "obscene" *Mistress Mine*. For Sophia has led no ordinary life, but has slaved and suffered—deliciously—under the hand of the notorious Mistress Malin. How long had she languished under the dominance of this incredible beauty? $4.95/109-8

LINDSAY WELSH

ROMANTIC ENCOUNTERS

Lindsay Welsh's most passionate story yet! Beautiful Julie, the most powerful editor of romance novels in the industry, spends her days igniting women's passions through books—and her nights fulfilling those needs with a variety of insatiable lovers. Slowly but surely, Julie's two world's come together with the type of bodice-ripping Harlequin could never imagine! $5.95/359-7

THE BEST OF LINDSAY WELSH

A collection of this popular writer's best work. This author was one of Rosebud's early bestsellers, and remains highly popular. A sampler set to introduce some of the hottest lesbian erotica to a wider audience. $5.95/368-6

PROVINCETOWN SUMMER

This completely original collection is devoted exclusively to white-hot desire between women. From the casual encounters of women on the prowl to the enduring erotic bonds between old lovers, the women of *Provincetown Summer* will set your senses on fire! A national best-seller. $5.95/362-7

ROSEBUD BOOKS

NECESSARY EVIL

What's a girl to do? When her Mistress proves too systematic, too by-the-book, one lovely submissive takes the ultimate chance—choosing and creating a Mistress who'll fulfill her heart's desire. Little did she know how difficult it would be—and, in the end, rewarding.... $5.95/277-9

A VICTORIAN ROMANCE

Lust-letters from the road. A young Englishwoman realizes her dream—a trip abroad under the guidance of her eccentric maiden aunt. Soon the young but blossoming Elaine comes to discover her own sexual talents, as a hot-blooded Parisian named Madelaine takes her Sapphic education in hand. Another Welsh winner! $5.95/365-1

A CIRCLE OF FRIENDS

The author of the nationally best-selling *Provincetown Summer* returns with the story of a remarkable group of women. Slowly, the women pair off to explore all the possibilities of lesbian passion, until finally it seems that there is nothing—and no one—they have not dabbled in. A stunning tribute to truly special relationships. $4.95/250-7

PRIVATE LESSONS

A high voltage tale of life at The Whitfield Academy for Young Women—where cruel headmistress Devon Whitfield presides over the in-depth education of only the most talented and delicious of maidens. Elizabeth Dunn arrives at the Academy, where it becomes clear that she has much to learn—to the delight of Devon Whitfield and her randy staff of Mistresses! Another contemporary classic from Lindsay Welsh. $4.95/116-0

BAD HABITS

What does one do with a poorly trained slave? Break her of her bad habits, of course! The story of the ultimate finishing school, *Bad Habits* was an immediate favorite with women nationwide. "Talk about passing the wet test!... If you like hot, lesbian erotica, run—don't walk...and pick up a copy of *Bad Habits*."—*Lambda Book Report* $4.95/3068-7

ANNABELLE BARKER

MOROCCO

A luscious young woman stands to inherit a fortune—if she can only withstand the ministrations of her cruel guardian until her twentieth birthday. With two months left, Lila makes a bold bid for freedom, only to find that liberty has its own excruciating and delicious price.... $4.95/148-9

A.L. REINE

DISTANT LOVE & OTHER STORIES

A book of seductive tales. In the title story, Leah Michaels and her lover Ranelle have had four years of blissful, smoldering passion together. One night, when Ranelle is out of town, Leah records an audio "Valentine", a cassette filled with erotic reminiscences.... $4.95/3056-3

RHINOCEROS BOOKS

BY HER SUBDUED

Stories of women who get what they want. The tales in this collection all involve women in control—of their lives, their loves, their men. So much in control, in fact, that they can remorselessly break rules to become the powerful goddesses of the men who sacrifice all to worship at their feet. Woman Power with a vengeance! $6.95/281-7

JEAN STINE

SEASON OF THE WITCH

"A future in which it is technically finally possible to transfer the total mind... of a rapist killer into the brain dead but physically living body of his female victim. Remarkable for intense psychological technique. There is eroticism but it is necessary to mark the differences between the sexes and the subtle altering of a man into a woman." —*The Science Fiction Critic* $6.95/268-X

JOHN WARREN

THE TORQUEMADA KILLER

Detective Eva Hernandez has finally gotten her first "big case": a string of vicious murders taking place within New York's SM community. Piece by piece, Eva assembles the evidence, revealing a picture of a world misunderstood and under attack—and gradually comes to understand her own place within it. A hot, edge-of-the-seat thriller from the author of *The Loving Dominant*—and an exciting insider's perspective on "the scene." $6.95/367-8

THE LOVING DOMINANT

Everything you need to know about an infamous sexual variation—and an unspoken type of love. Mentor—a longtime player in the dominance/submission scene—guides readers through this world and reveals the too-often hidden basis of the D/S relationship: care, trust and love. $6.95/218-3

GRANT ANTREWS

SUBMISSIONS

Once again, Antrews portrays the very special elements of the dominant/submissive relationship...with restraint—this time with the story of a lonely man, a winning lottery ticket, and a demanding dominatrix. One of erotica's most discerning writers. $6.95/207-8

MY DARLING DOMINATRIX

When a man and a woman fall in love it's supposed to be simple, uncomplicated, easy—unless that woman happens to be a dominatrix. Curiosity gives way to unblushing desire in this story of one man's awakening to the joys to be experienced as the willing slave of a powerful woman. $6.95/3055-5

LAURA ANTONIOU WRITING AS "SARA ADAMSON"

THE TRAINER

The long-awaited conclusion of Adamson's stunning Marketplace Trilogy! The ultimate underground sexual realm includes not only willing slaves, but the exquisite trainers who take submissives firmly in hand. And it is now the time for these mentors to divulge their own secrets—the desires that led them to become the ultimate figures of authority. $6.95/249-3

THE SLAVE

The second volume in the "Marketplace" trilogy. *The Slave* covers the experience of one exceptionally talented submissive who longs to join the ranks of those who have proven themselves worthy of entry into the Marketplace. But the price, while delicious, is staggeringly high.... Adamson's plot thickens, as her trilogy moves to a conclusion in *The Trainer*. $6.95/173-X

RHINOCEROS BOOKS

THE MARKETPLACE

"Merchandise does not come easily to the Marketplace.... They haunt the clubs and the organizations.... Some of them are so ripe that they intimidate the poseurs, the weekend sadists and the furtive dilettantes who are so endemic to that world. And they never stop asking where we may be found...." $6.95/3096-2

THE CATALYST

After viewing a controversial, explicitly kinky film full of images of bondage and submission, several audience members find themselves deeply moved by the erotic suggestions they've seen on the screen. "Sara Adamson"'s sensational debut volume! $5.95/328-7

DAVID AARON CLARK

SISTER RADIANCE

A chronicle of obsession, rife with Clark's trademark vivisections of contemporary desires, sacred and profane. The vicissitudes of lust and romance are examined against a backdrop of urban decay and shallow fashionability in this testament to the allure—and inevitability—of the forbidden. $6.95/215-9

THE WET FOREVER

The story of Janus and Madchen, a small-time hood and a beautiful sex worker, *The Wet Forever* examines themes of loyalty, sacrifice, redemption and obsession amidst Manhattan's sex parlors and underground S/M clubs. Its combination of sex and suspense led Terence Sellers to proclaim it "evocative and poetic." $6.95/117-9

ALICE JOANOU

BLACK TONGUE

"Joanou has created a series of sumptuous, brooding, dark visions of sexual obsession and is undoubtedly a name to look out for in the future."
—*Redeemer*

Another seductive book of dreams from the author of the acclaimed *Tourniquet*. Exploring lust at its most florid and unsparing, *Black Tongue* is a trove of baroque fantasies—each redolent of the forbidden. Joanou creates some of erotica's most mesmerizing and unforgettable characters. A critical favorite. $6.95/258-2

TOURNIQUET

A heady collection of stories and effusions from the pen of one our most dazzling young writers. Strange tales abound, from the story of the mysterious and cruel Cybele, to an encounter with the sadistic entertainment of a bizarre after-hours cafe. A sumptuous feast for all the senses.. $6.95/3060-1

CANNIBAL FLOWER

"She is waiting in her darkened bedroom, as she has waited throughout history, to seduce the men who are foolish enough to be blinded by her irresistible charms....She is the goddess of sexuality, and *Cannibal Flower* is her haunting siren song."—Michael Perkins $4.95/72-6

MICHAEL PERKINS

EVIL COMPANIONS

Set in New York City during the tumultuous waning years of the Sixties, *Evil Companions* has been hailed as "a frightening classic." A young couple explores the nether reaches of the erotic unconscious in a shocking confrontation with the extremes of passion. With a new introduction by science fiction legend Samuel R. Delany. $6.95/3067-9

RHINOCEROS BOOKS

AN ANTHOLOGY OF CLASSIC ANONYMOUS EROTIC WRITING

Michael Perkins, acclaimed authority on erotic literature, has collected the very best passages from the world's erotic writing—especially for Rhino*ceros* readers. "Anonymous" is one of the most infamous bylines in publishing history—and these steamy excerpts show why! $6.95/140-3

THE SECRET RECORD: Modern Erotic Literature

Michael Perkins, a renowned author and critic of sexually explicit fiction, surveys the field with authority and unique insight. Updated and revised to include the latest trends, tastes, and developments in this misunderstood and maligned genre. An important volume for every erotic reader and fan of high quality adult fiction. $6.95/3039-3

HELEN HENLEY

ENTER WITH TRUMPETS

Helen Henley was told that woman just don't write about sex—much less the taboos she was so interested in exploring. So Henley did it alone, flying in the face of "tradition" by producing *Enter With Trumpets*, a touching tale of arousal and devotion in one couple's kinky relationship. $6.95/197-7

PHILIP JOSE FARMER

FLESH

Space Commander Stagg explored the galaxies for 800 years. Upon his return, the hero Stagg is made the centerpiece of an incredible public ritual—one that will repeatedly take him to the heights of ecstasy, and inexorably drag him toward the depths of hell. $6.95/303-1

A FEAST UNKNOWN

"Sprawling, brawling, shocking, suspenseful, hilarious…"

—Theodore Sturgeon

Farmer's supreme anti-hero returns. *A Feast Unknown* begins in 1968, with Lord Grandrith's stunning statement: "I was conceived and born in 1888." Slowly, Lord Grandrith—armed with the belief that he is the son of Jack the Ripper—tells the story of his remarkable and unbridled life. Beginning with his discovery of the secret of immortality, Grandrith's tale proves him no raving lunatic—but something far more bizarre…. $6.95/276-0

THE IMAGE OF THE BEAST

Herald Childe has seen Hell, glimpsed its horror in an act of sexual mutilation. Childe must now find and destroy an inhuman predator through the streets of a polluted and decadent Los Angeles of the future. One clue after another leads Childe to an inescapable realization about the nature of sex and evil…. $6.95/166-7

SAMUEL R. DELANY

EQUINOX

The *Scorpion* has sailed the seas in a quest for every possible pleasure. Her crew is a collection of the young, the twisted, the insatiable. A drifter comes into their midst, and is taken on a fantastic journey to the darkest, most dangerous sexual extremes—until he is finally a victim to their boundless appetites. $6.95/157-8

DANIEL VIAN

ILLUSIONS

Two tales of danger and desire in Berlin on the eve of WWII. From private homes to lurid cafés, passion is exposed and explored in stark contrast to the brutal violence of the time. A singularly arousing volume. $6.95/3074-1

RHINOCEROS BOOKS

PERSUASIONS

"The stockings are drawn tight by the suspender belt, tight enough to be stretched to the limit just above the middle part of her thighs..." A double novel, including the classics *Adagio* and *Gabriela and the General*, this volume traces desire around the globe. International lust! $6.95/183-7

ANDREI CODRESCU

THE REPENTANCE OF LORRAINE

"One of our most prodigiously talented and magical writers."
—*NYT Book Review*

An aspiring writer, a professor's wife, a secretary, gold anklets, Maoists, Roman harlots—and more—swirl through this spicy tale of a harried quest for a mythic artifact. Written when the author was a young man, this lusty yarn was inspired by the heady days of the Sixties. Includes a new Introduction by the author, painting a portrait of *Lorraine*'s creation. $6.95/329-5

LEOPOLD VON SACHER-MASOCH

VENUS IN FURS

This classic 19th century novel is the first uncompromising exploration of the dominant/submissive relationship in literature. The alliance of Severin and Wanda epitomizes Sacher-Masoch's dark obsession with a cruel, controlling goddess and the urges that drive the man held in her thrall. Includes the letters exchanged between Sacher-Masoch and Emilie Mataja—an aspiring writer he sought as the avatar of his forbidden desires. $6.95/3089-X

SOPHIE GALLEYMORE BIRD

MANEATER

Through a bizarre act of creation, a man attains the "perfect" lover—by all appearances a beautiful, sensuous woman but in reality something far darker. Once brought to life she will accept no mate, seeking instead the prey that will sate her hunger for vengeance. A biting take on the war of the sexes, this debut goes for the jugular of the "perfect woman" myth. $6.95/103-9

TUPPY OWENS

SENSATIONS

A piece of porn history. Tuppy Owens tells the unexpurgated story of the making of *Sensations*—the first big-budget sex flick. Originally commissioned to appear in book form after the release of the film in 1975, *Sensations* is finally released under Masquerade's stylish Rhinoceros imprint. $6.95/3081-4

LIESEL KULIG

LOVE IN WARTIME

An uncompromising look at the politics, perils and pleasures of sexual power. Madeleine knew that the handsome SS officer was a dangerous man. But she was just a cabaret singer in Nazi-occupied Paris, trying to survive in a perilous time. When Josef fell in love with her, he discovered that a beautiful and amoral woman can sometimes be wildly dangerous. $6.95/3044-X

MASQUERADE BOOKS

COMPLIANCE   *N. Whallen*
A collection of fourteen stories exploring the pleasures of release. Characters from many walks of life learn to trust in the skills of others, only to experience the thrilling liberation of submission. No other book so clearly depicts the real joys to be found in some of the most forbidden sexual practices around....
$5.95/356-2

LA DOMME: A DOMINATRIX ANTHOLOGY   *Edited by Claire Baeder*
A steamy smorgasbord of female domination! Erotic literature has long been filled with heartstopping portraits of domineering women, and now the most memorable come together in one beautifully brutal volume. No fan of real woman power can afford to miss this ultimate compendium. $5.95/366-X

THE GEEK   *Tiny Alice*
"An adventure novel told by a sex-bent male mini-pygmy. This is an accomplishment of which anybody may be proud."

—Philip José Farmer

A notorious cult classic. *The Geek* is told from the point of view of, well, a chicken who reports on the various perversities he witnesses as part of a traveling carnival. When a gang of renegade lesbians kidnaps Chicken and his geek, all hell breaks loose. A strange tale, filled with outrageous erotic oddities, that finally returns to print after years of infamy. $5.95/341-4

SEX ON THE NET   *Charisse van der Lyn*
Electrifying erotica from one of the Internet's hottest and most widely read authors. Encounters of all kinds—straight, lesbian, dominant/submissive and all sorts of extreme passions—are explored in thrilling detail. Discover what's turning on hackers from coast to coast! $5.95/399-6

BEAUTY OF THE BEAST   *Carole Remy*
A shocking tell-all, written from the point-of-view of a prize-winning reporter. And what reporting she does! All the secrets of an uninhibited life are revealed, and each lusty tableau is painted in glowing colors. Join in on her scandalous adventures—and reap the rewards of her extensive background in Erotic Affairs! $5.95/332-5

NAUGHTY MESSAGE   *Stanley Carten*
Wesley Arthur, a withdrawn computer engineer, discovers a lascivious message on his answering machine. Aroused beyond his wildest dreams by the unmentionable acts described, Wesley becomes obsessed with tracking down the woman behind the seductive voice. His search takes him through strip clubs and no-tell motels—and finally to his randy reward.... $5.95/333-3

The Marquis de Sade's JULIETTE   *David Aaron Clark*
The Marquis de Sade's infamous Juliette returns—and at the hand of David Aaron Clark, she emerges as the most powerful, perverse and destructive nightstalker modern New York will ever know. Under this domina's tutelage, two women come to know torture's bizarre attractions, as they grapple with the price of Juliette's promise of immortality.
Praise for Dave Clark:
"David Aaron Clark has delved into one of the most sensationalistically taboo aspects of eros, sadomasochism, and produced a novel of unmistakable literary imagination and artistic value."   —Carlo McCormick, *Paper*
$5.95/240-X

THE PARLOR   *N.T. Morley*
Lovely Kathryn gives in to the ultimate temptation. The mysterious John and Sarah ask her to be their slave—an idea that turns Kathryn on so much that she can't refuse! But who are these two mysterious strangers? Little by little, Kathryn comes to know the inner secrets of her stunning keepers. Soon, all is revealed—to the delight of everyone involved! $5.95/291-4

MASQUERADE BOOKS

NADIA *Anonymous*

"Nadia married General the Count Gregorio Stenoff—a gentleman of noble pedigree it is true, but one of the most reckless dissipated rascals in Russia..." Follow the delicious but neglected Nadia as she works to wring every drop of pleasure out of life—despite an unhappy marriage. A classic title providing a peek into the secret sexual lives of another time and place. $5.95/267-1

THE STORY OF A VICTORIAN MAID *Nigel McParr*

What were the Victorians really like? Chances are, no one believes they were as stuffy as their Queen, but who would have imagined such unbridled libertines! One maid is followed from exploit to smutty exploit, and all secrets are revealed! $5.95/241-8

CARRIE'S STORY *Molly Weatherfield*

"I had been Jonathan's slave for about a year when he told me he wanted to sell me at an auction. I wasn't in any condition to respond when he told me this..." Desire and depravity run rampant in this story of uncompromising mastery and irrevocable submission. $5.95/228-0

CHARLY'S GAME *Bren Flemming*

Charly's a no-nonsense private detective facing the fight of her life. A rich woman's gullible daughter has run off with one of the toughest leather dykes in town—and Charly's hired to lure the girl back. One by one, wise and wicked women ensnare one another in their lusty nets! $4.95/221-3

ANDREA AT THE CENTER *J.P. Kansas*

Lithe and lovely young Andrea is, without warning, whisked away to a distant retreat. There she is introduced to the ways of the Center, and soon becomes quite friendly with its other inhabitants—all of whom are learning to abandon restraint in their pursuit of the deepest sexual satisfaction. $5.95/324-4

ASK ISADORA *Isadora Alman*

An essential volume, collecting six years' worth of Isadora Alman's syndicated columns on sex and relationships. Alman's been called a "hip Dr. Ruth," and a "sexy Dear Abby," based upon the wit and pertinence of her advice. Today's world is more perplexing than ever—and Isadora Alman is just the expert to help untangle the most personal of knots. $4.95/61-0

THE SLAVES OF SHOANNA *Mercedes Kelly*

Shoanna, the cruel and magnificent, takes four maidens under her wing—and teaches them the ins and outs of pleasure and discipline. Trained in every imaginable perversion, from simple fleshly joys to advanced techniques, these students go to the head of the class! $4.95/164-0

LOVE & SURRENDER *Marlene Darcy*

"Madeline saw Harry looking at her legs and she blushed as she remembered what he wanted to do.... She casually pulled the skirt of her dress back to uncover her knees and the lower part of her thighs. What did he want now? Did he want more? She tugged at her skirt again, pulled it back far enough so almost all of her thighs were exposed...." $4.95/3082-2

THE COMPLETE *PLAYGIRL* FANTASIES *Editors of* Playgirl

The best women's fantasies are collected here, fresh from the pages of *Playgirl*. These knockouts from the infamous "Reader's Fantasy Forum" prove, once again, that truth can indeed be hotter, wilder, and *better* than fiction. $4.95/3075-X

STASI SLUT *Anthony Bobarzynski*

Need we say more? Adina lives in East Germany, far from the sexually liberated, uninhibited debauchery of the West. She meets a group of ruthless and corrupt STASI agents who use her as a pawn in their political chess game as well as for their own perverse gratification— until she uses her talents and attractions in a final bid for total freedom! $4.95/3050-4

MASQUERADE BOOKS

BLUE TANGO
Hilary Manning

Ripe and tempting Julie is haunted by the sounds of extraordinary passion beyond her bedroom wall. Alone, she fantasizes about taking part in the amorous dramas of her hosts, Claire and Edward. When she finds a way to watch the nightly debauch, her curiosity turns to full-blown lust—and soon Julie's eager to join in! $4.95/3037-7

LOUISE BELHAVEL

FRAGRANT ABUSES

The saga of Clara and Iris continues as the now-experienced girls enjoy themselves with a new circle of worldly friends whose imaginations match their own. Perversity follows the lusty ladies around the globe! $4.95/88-2

DEPRAVED ANGELS

The final installment in the incredible adventures of Clara and Iris. Together with their friends, lovers, and worldly acquaintances, Clara and Iris explore the frontiers of depravity at home and abroad. $4.95/92-0

TITIAN BERESFORD

THE WICKED HAND

With a special Introduction by *Leg Show*'s Dian Hanson. A collection of fanciful fetishistic tales featuring the absolute subjugation of men by lovely, domineering women. From Japan and Germany to the American heartland—these stories uncover the other side of the "weaker sex." Another bonanza for Beresford fans! $5.95/343-0

CINDERELLA

Beresford triumphs again with this intoxicating tale, filled with castle dungeons and tightly corseted ladies-in-waiting, naughty viscounts and impossibly cruel masturbatrixes—nearly every conceivable method of erotic torture is explored and described in lush, vivid detail. $4.95/305-8

JUDITH BOSTON

Young Edward would have been lucky to get the stodgy old companion he thought his parents had hired for him. Instead, an exquisite woman arrives at his door, and Edward finds his compulsively lewd behavior never goes unpunished by the unflinchingly severe Judith Boston! A bona fide classic, and one of our most requested titles. $4.95/273-6

NINA FOXTON

An aristocrat finds herself bored by run-of-the-mill amusements for "ladies of good breeding." Instead of taking tea with proper gentlemen, naughty Nina invents a contraption to "milk" them of their most private essences. No man ever says "No" to Nina! $4.95/145-4

A TITIAN BERESFORD READER

Beresford's fanciful settings and outrageous fetishism have established his reputation as modern erotica's most imaginative and spirited writer. Wild dominatrixes, perverse masochists, and mesmerizing detail are the hallmarks of the Beresford tale—and encountered here in abundance. The very best scenarios from all of Beresford's bestsellers. Makes this a must-have for the Compleat Fetishist. $4.95/114-4

CHINA BLUE

KUNG FU NUNS

"When I could stand the pleasure no longer, she lifted me out of the chair and sat me down on top of the table. She then lifted her skirt. The sight of her perfect legs clad in white stockings and a petite garter belt further mesmerized me. I lean particularly towards white garter belts." China Blue returns! $4.95/3031-8

MASQUERADE BOOKS

HARRIET DAIMLER

DARLING • INNOCENCE

In *Darling*, a virgin is raped by a mugger. Driven by her urge for revenge, she searches New York in a furious sexual hunt that leads to rape and murder. In *Innocence*, a young invalid determines to experience sex through her voluptuous nurse. Two critically acclaimed novels. $4.95/3047-4

AKBAR DEL PIOMBO

SKIRTS

Randy Mr. Edward Champdick enters high society—and a whole lot more—in his quest for ultimate satisfaction. For it seems that once Mr. Champdick rises to the occasion, nothing can bring him down. $4.95/115-2

DUKE COSIMO

A kinky romp played out against the boudoirs, bathrooms and ballrooms of the European nobility, who seem to do nothing all day except each other. The lifestyles of the rich and licentious are revealed in all their glory. Lust-styles of the rich and infamous! $4.95/3052-0

A CRUMBLING FAÇADE

The return of that incorrigible rogue, Henry Pike, who continues his pursuit of sex, fair or otherwise, in the most elegant homes of the most debauched aristocrats. No one can resist the irrepressible Pike! $4.95/3043-1

PAULA

"How bad do you want me?" she asked, her voice husky, breathy. I shrank back, for my desire for her was swelling to unspeakable proportions. "Turn around," she said, and I obeyed....This canny seductress tests the mettle of every man who comes under her spell—and every man does! $4.95/3036-9

ROBERT DESMOND

PROFESSIONAL CHARMER

A gigolo lives a parasitical life of luxury by providing his sexual services to the rich and bored. Traveling in the most exclusive circles, this gun-for-hire will gratify the lewdest and most vulgar sexual cravings! This dedicated pro leaves no one unsatisfied. $4.95/3003-2

THE SWEETEST FRUIT

Connie is determined to seduce and destroy Father Chadcroft. She corrupts the unsuspecting priest into forsaking all that he holds sacred, destroys his parish, and slyly manipulates him with her smoldering looks and hypnotic aura. $4.95/95-5

MICHAEL DRAX

SILK AND STEEL

"He stood tall and strong in the shadows of her room... Akemi knew what he was there for. He let his robe fall to the floor. She could offer no resistance as the shadowy figure knelt before her, gazing down upon her. Why would she resist? This was what she wanted all along...." $4.95/3032-6

OBSESSIONS

Victoria is determined to become a model by sexually ensnaring the powerful people who control the fashion industry: Paige, who finds herself compelled to watch Victoria's conquests; and Pietro and Alex, who take turns and then join in for a sizzling threesome. $4.95/3012-1

LIZBETH DUSSEAU

TRINKETS

"Her bottom danced on the air, pert and fully round. It would take punishment well, he thought." A luscious woman submits to an artist's every whim—becoming the sexual trinket he had always desired. $5.95/246-9

MASQUERADE BOOKS

CANDY LIPS

The world of publishing serves as the backdrop for one woman's pursuit of sexual satisfaction. From a fiery femme fatale to a voracious Valentino, she takes her pleasure where she can find it. Luckily for her, it's most often found between the legs of the most licentious lovers! $4.95/182-9

KIM'S PASSION

The life of a beautiful English seductress. Kim leaves India for London, where she quickly takes upon herself the task of bedding every woman in sight! One by one, the lovely Kim's conquests accumulate, until she finds herself in the arms of gentry and commoners alike. $4.95/162-4

CAROUSEL

A young American woman leaves her husband when she discovers he is having an affair with their maid. She then becomes the sexual plaything of various Parisian voluptuaries. Wild sex, low morals, and ultimate decadence in the flamboyant years before the European collapse. $4.95/3051-2

SABINE

There is no one who can refuse her once she casts her spell; no lover can do anything less than give up his whole life for her. Great men and empires fall at her feet; but she is haughty, distracted, impervious. It is the eve of WW II, and Sabine must find a new lover equal to her talents. $4.95/3046-6

THE WILD HEART

A luxury hotel is the setting for this artful web of sex, desire, and love. A newlywed sees sex as a duty, while her hungry husband tries to awaken her to its tender joys. A Parisian entertains wealthy guests for the love of money. Each episode provides a new variation in this lusty Grand Hotel! $4.95/3007-5

JADE EAST

Laura, passive and passionate, follows her husband Emilio to Hong Kong. He gives her to Wu Li, a connoisseur of sexual perversions, who passes her on to Madeleine, a flamboyant lesbian. Madeleine's friends make Laura the centerpiece in Hong Kong's infamous underground orgies. Slowly, Laura descends into the depths of depravity. Steamy slaves—for sale! $4.95/60-2

RAWHIDE LUST

Diana Beaumont, the young wife of a U.S. Marshal, is kidnapped as an act of vengeance against her husband. Jack Beaumont sets out on a long journey to get his wife back, but finally catches up with her trail only to learn that she's been sold into white slavery in Mexico. $4.95/55-6

THE JAZZ AGE

The time: the Roaring Twenties. A young attorney becomes suspicious of his mistress while his wife has an fling with a lesbian lover. *The Jazz Age* is a romp of erotic realism from the heyday of the speakeasy. $4.95/48-3

AMARANTHA KNIGHT

THE DARKER PASSIONS:
THE FALL OF THE HOUSE OF USHER

The Master and Mistress of the house of Usher indulge in every form of decadence, and are intent on initiating their guests into the many pleasures to be found in utter submission. But something is not quite right in the House of Usher, and the foundation of its dynasty begins to crack.... $5.95/313-9

THE DARKER PASSIONS: *FRANKENSTEIN*

What if you could create a living, breathing human? What shocking acts could it be taught to perform, to desire, to love? Find out what pleasures await those who play God.... $5.95/248-5

MASQUERADE BOOKS

TUTORED IN LUST

This tale of the initiation and instruction of a carnal college co-ed and her fellow students unlocks the sex secrets of the classroom. Books take a back seat to secret societies and their bizarre ceremonies in this story of students with an unquenchable thirst for knowledge! $4.95/78-5

DANGEROUS LESSONS

A compendium of corporeal punishment from the twisted mind of bestselling Paul Little. Incredibly arousing morsels abound: *Tears of the Inquisition, Lust of the Cossacks, Poor Darlings, Captive Maidens, Slave Island*, even the scandalous *The Metamorphosis of Lisette Joyaux*. $4.95/32-7

THE LUSTFUL TURK

The majestic ruler of Algiers and a modest English virgin face off—to their mutual delight. Emily Bartow is initially horrified by the unrelenting sexual tortures to be endured under the powerful Turk's hand. But soon she comes to crave her debasement—no matter what the cost! $4.95/163-2

TEARS OF THE INQUISITION

The incomparable Paul Little delivers a staggering account of pleasure and punishment. *"There was a tickling inside her as her nervous system reminded her she was ready for sex. But before her was...the Inquisitor!"* Unquestionable, one of Little's most torturous titles. $4.95/146-2

DOUBLE NOVEL

Two of Paul Little's bestselling novels in one spellbinding volume! *The Metamorphosis of Lisette Joyaux* tells the story of an innocent young woman initiated into a new world of lesbian lusts. *The Story of Monique* reveals the sexual rituals that beckon the ripe and willing Monique. $4.95/86-6

CHINESE JUSTICE AND OTHER STORIES

Chinese Justice is already a classic—the story of the excruciating pleasures and delicious punishments inflicted on foreigners under the tyrannical leaders of the Boxer Rebellion. One by one, each foreign woman is brought before the authorities and grilled. Scandalous tortures are inflicted upon the helpless females by their relentless, merciless captors. $4.95/153-5

SLAVES OF CAMEROON

This sordid tale is about the women who were used by German officers for salacious profit. These women were forced to become whores for the German army in this African colony. The most perverse forms of erotic gratification are depicted in this unsavory tale of women exploited in every way possible. One of Paul Little's most infamous titles. $4.95/3026-1

ALL THE WAY

Two excruciating novels from Paul Little in one hot volume! *Going All the Way* features an unhappy man who tries to purge himself of the memory of his lover with a series of quirky and uninhibited women. *Pushover* tells the story of a serial spanker and his celebrated exploits in California. $4.95/3023-7

CAPTIVE MAIDENS

Three beautiful young women find themselves powerless against the wealthy, debauched landowners of 1824 England. They are banished to a sexual slave colony, and corrupted by every imaginable perversion. $4.95/3014-8

SLAVE ISLAND

A leisure cruise is waylaid, finding itself in the domain of Lord Henry Philbrock, a sadistic genius, who has built a hidden paradise where captive females are forced into slavery. The ship's passengers are kidnapped and spirited to his island prison, where the women are trained to accommodate the most bizarre sexual cravings of the rich, the famous, the pampered and the perverted. One of our hottest-selling titles. $4.95/3006-7

MASQUERADE BOOKS

SYDNEY ST. JAMES

RIVE GAUCHE

Decadence and debauchery among the doomed artists in the Latin Quarter, Paris circa 1920. Expatriate bohemians couple with abandon—before eventually abandoning their ambitions amidst the intoxicating temptations waiting to be indulged in every bedroom. $5.95/317-1

THE HIGHWAYWOMAN

A young filmmaker making a documentary about the life of the notorious English highwaywoman, Bess Ambrose, becomes obsessed with her mysterious subject. It seems that Bess touched more than hearts—and plundered the treasures of every man and maiden she met on the way. $4.95/174-8

GARDEN OF DELIGHT

A vivid account of sexual awakening that follows an innocent but insatiably curious young woman's journey from the furtive, forbidden joys of dormitory life to the unabashed carnality of the wild world. Pretty Pauline blossoms with each new experiment in the sensual arts. $4.95/3058-X

ALEXANDER TROCCHI

THONGS

"...In Spain, life is cheap, from that glittering tragedy in the bullring to the quick thrust of the stiletto in a narrow street in a Barcelona slum. No, this death would not have called for further comment had it not been for one striking fact. The naked woman had met her end in a way he had never seen before—a way that had enormous sexual significance. My God, she had been..." $4.95/217-5

HELEN AND DESIRE

Helen Seferis' flight from the oppressive village of her birth became a sexual tour of a harsh world. From brothels in Sydney to harems in Algiers, Helen chronicles her adventures fully in her diary. Each encounter is examined in the scorching and uncensored diary of the sensual Helen! $4.95/3093-8

THE CARNAL DAYS OF HELEN SEFERIS

Private Investigator Anthony Harvest is assigned to save Helen Seferis, a beautiful Australian who has been abducted. Following clues in Helen's explicit diary of adventures, he Helen, the ultimate sexual prize. $4.95/3086-5

WHITE THIGHS

A fantasy of obsession from a modern erotic master. This is the story of Saul and his sexual fixation on the beautiful, tormented Anna. Their scorching passion leads to murder and madness every time. $4.95/3009-1

SCHOOL FOR SIN

When Peggy leaves her country home behind for the bright lights of Dublin, her sensuous nature leads to her seduction by a stranger. He recruits her into a training school where no one knows what awaits them at graduation, but each student is sure to be well schooled in sex! $4.95/ 89-0

MY LIFE AND LOVES (THE 'LOST' VOLUME)

What happens when you try to fake a sequel to the most scandalous autobiography of the 20th century? If the "forgers" are two of the most important figures in modern erotica, you get a masterpiece, and THIS IS IT! One of the most thrilling forgeries in literature. $4.95/52-1

MARCUS VAN HELLER

TERROR

Another shocking exploration of lust by the author of the ever-popular *Adam & Eve*. Set in Paris during the Algerian War, *Terror* explores the place of sexual passion in a world drunk on violence. $5.95/247-7

MASQUERADE BOOKS

KIDNAP

Private Investigator Harding is called in to investigate a mysterious kidnapping case involving the rich and powerful. Along the way he has the pleasure of "interrogating" an exotic dancer named Jeanne and a beautiful English reporter, as he finds himself enmeshed in the crime underworld. $4.95/90-4

LUSCIDIA WALLACE

KATY'S AWAKENING

Katy thinks she's been rescued after a terrible car wreck. Little does she suspect that she's been ensnared by a ring of swingers whose tastes run to domination and unimaginably depraved sex parties. With no means of escape, Katy becomes the newest initiate into this sick private club—much to her pleasure! $4.95/308-2

FOR SALE BY OWNER

Susie was overwhelmed by the lavishness of the yacht, the glamour of the guests. But she didn't know the plans they had for her: Sexual torture, training and sale into slavery! How many maids had been lured onto this floating prison? And how many gave as much pleasure as the newly wicked Susie? Unspeakable ravishments abound in this tale of the ultimate sex cruise—from which no one escapes! $4.95/3064-4

THE ICE MAIDEN

Edward Canton has ruthlessly seized everything he wants in life, with one exception: Rebecca Esterbrook. Frustrated by his inability to seduce her with money, he kidnaps her and whisks her away to his remote island compound, where she emerges as a writhing, red-hot love slave! $4.95/3001-6

DON WINSLOW

THE MANY PLEASURES OF IRONWOOD

Seven lovely young women are employed by The Ironwood Sportsmen's club for the entertainment of gentlemen. A small and exclusive club with seven carefully selected sexual connoisseurs, Ironwood is dedicated to the relentless pursuit of sensual pleasure. $5.95/310-4

CLAIRE'S GIRLS

You knew when she walked by that she was something special. She was one of Claire's girls, a woman carefully dressed and groomed to fill a role, to capture a look, to fit an image crafted by the sophisticated proprietress of an exclusive escort agency. High-class whores blow the roof off! $4.95/108-X

GLORIA'S INDISCRETION

"He looked up at her. Gloria stood passively, her hands loosely at her sides, her eyes still closed, a dreamy expression on her face ... She sensed his hungry eyes on her, could almost feel his burning gaze on her body...." $4.95/3094-6

THE MASQUERADE READERS

THE COMPLETE EROTIC READER

The very best in erotic writing together in a wicked collection sure to stimulate even the most jaded and "sophisticated" palates. $4.95/3063-6

THE VELVET TONGUE

An orgy of oral gratification! *The Velvet Tongue* celebrates the most mouth-watering, lip-smacking, tongue-twisting action. A feast of fellatio and *soixante-neuf* awaits readers of excellent taste at this steamy suck-fest. $4.95/3029-6

A MASQUERADE READER

Strict lessons are learned at the hand of *The English Governess*. Scandalous confessions are found in *The Diary of an Angel*, and the story of a woman whose desires drove her to the ultimate sacrifice in *Thongs* completes the collection. $4.95/84-X

MASQUERADE BOOKS

THE CLASSIC COLLECTION

SCHOOL DAYS IN PARIS

The rapturous chronicles of a well-spent youth! Few Universities provide the profound and pleasurable lessons one learns in after-hours study—particularly if one is young and available, and lucky enough to have Paris as a playground. A stimulating look at the pursuits of young adulthood. $5.95/325-2

MAN WITH A MAID

The adventures of Jack and Alice have delighted readers for eight decades! A classic of its genre, *Man with a Maid* tells an outrageous tale of desire, revenge, and submission. Over 200,000 copies in print! $4.95/307-4

MAN WITH A MAID II

Jack's back! With the assistance of the perverse Alice, he embarks again on a trip through every erotic extreme. Jack leaves no one unsatisfied—least of all, himself, and Alice is always certain to outdo herself in her capacity to corrupt and control. An incendiary sequel! $4.95/3071-7

MAN WITH A MAID: The Conclusion

The final chapter in the epic saga of lust that has thrilled readers for decades. The adulterous woman who is corrected with enthusiasm and the maid who receives grueling guidance are just two who benefit from these lessons! Don't miss this conclusion to erotica's most famous tale. $4.95/3013-X

CONFESSIONS OF A CONCUBINE III: PLEASURE'S PRISONER

The further adventures of erotica's most famous concubine! Filled with pulse-pounding excitement—including a daring escape from the harem and an encounter with an unspeakable sadist—*Pleasure's Prisoner* adds an unforget-table chapter to this thrilling confessional. $5.95/357-0

CONFESSIONS OF A CONCUBINE II: HAREM SLAVE

The concubinage continues, as the true pleasures and privileges of the harem are revealed. For the first time, readers are invited behind the veils that hide uninhibited, unimaginable pleasures from the world.... $4.95/226-4

CONFESSIONS OF A CONCUBINE

What *really* happens behind the plush walls of the harem? An inexperienced woman, captured and sentenced to service the royal pleasure, tells all in an outrageously unre-strained memoir. No affairs of state could match the passions of a young woman learning to relish a life of ceaseless sexual servitude. $4.95/154-3

INITIATION RITES

Every naughty detail of a young woman's breaking in! Under the thorough tutelage of the perverse Miss Clara Birchem, Julia learns her wicked lessons well. During the course of her amorous studies, the resourceful young lady is joined by an assortment of lewd characters. $4.95/120-9

TABLEAUX VIVANTS

Fifteen breathtaking tales of erotic passion. Upstanding ladies and gents soon adopt more comfortable positions, as wicked thoughts explode into sinfully scrumptious acts. Carnal extremes and explorations abound in this tribute to the spirit of Eros—the lustiest common denominator! $4.95/121-7

LADY F.

An uncensored tale of Victorian passions. Master Kidrodstock suffers deli-ciously at the hands of the stunningly cruel and sensuous Lady Flayskin—the only woman capable of taming his wayward impulses. $4.95/102-0

SACRED PASSIONS

Young Augustus comes into the heavenly sanctuary seeking protection from the enemies of his debt-ridden father. Within these walls he learns lessons he could never have imagined and soon concludes that the joys of the body far surpass those of the spirit. $4.95/21-1

MASQUERADE BOOKS

CLASSIC EROTIC BIOGRAPHIES

JENNIFER III

The further adventures of erotica's most daring heroine. Jennifer, the quintessential beautiful blonde, has a photographer's eye for detail—particularly details of the masculine variety! A raging nymphomaniac! $5.95/292-2

JENNIFER AGAIN

One of contemporary erotica's hottest characters returns, in a sequel sure to blow you away. Once again, the insatiable Jennifer seizes the day—and extracts from it every last drop of sensual pleasure! $4.95/220-5

JENNIFER

From the bedroom of an internationally famous—and notoriously insatiable—dancer to an uninhibited ashram, *Jennifer* traces the exploits of one thoroughly modern woman. $4.95/107-1

ROSEMARY LANE *J.D. Hall*

The ups, downs, ins and outs of Rosemary Lane. Raised as the ward of Lord and Lady D'Arcy, after coming of age she discovers that her guardians' generosity is boundless—as they contribute to her carnal education! $4.95/3078-4

THE ROMANCES OF BLANCHE LA MARE

When Blanche loses her husband, it becomes clear she'll need a job. She sets her sights on the stage—and soon encounters a cast of lecherous characters intent on making her path to sucksess as hot and hard as possible! $4.95/101-2

KATE PERCIVAL

Kate, the "Belle of Delaware," divulges the secrets of her scandalous life, from her earliest sexual experiments to the deviations she learns to love. Nothing is secret, and no holes barred in this titillating tell-all. $4.95/3072-5

THE AMERICAN COLLECTION

LUST *Palmiro Vicarion*

A wealthy and powerful man of leisure recounts his rise up the corporate ladder and his corresponding descent into debauchery. A tale of a classic scoundrel with an uncurbed appetite for sexual power! $4.95/82-3

WAYWARD *Peter Jason*

A mysterious countess hires a tour bus for an unusual vacation. Traveling through Europe's most notorious cities, she picks up friends, lovers, and acquaintances from every walk of life in pursuit of pleasure. $4.95/3004-0

LOVE'S ILLUSION

Elizabeth Renard yearned for the body of Dan Harrington. Then she discovers Harrington's secret weakness: a need to be humiliated and punished. She makes him her slave, and together they commence a journey into depravity that leaves nothing to the imagination—*nothing!* $4.95/100-4

THE RELUCTANT CAPTIVE

Kidnapped by ruthless outlaws who kill her husband and burn their prosperous ranch, Sarah's journey takes her from the bordellos of the Wild West to the bedrooms of Boston, where she's bought by a stranger from her past. $4.95/3022-9

A RICHARD KASAK BOOK

CECILIA TAN, EDITOR

SM VISIONS

"Fabulous books! There's nothing else like them."

—Susie Bright, *Best American Erotica* and *Herotica 3*.

A volume of the very best speculative erotica available today. Circlet Press, the first publishing house to devote itself exclusively to the erotic science fiction and fantasy genre, is now represented by the best of its very best: *SM Visions*—sure to be one of the most thrilling and eye-opening rides through the erotic imagination ever published. $12.95/339-2

FELICE PICANO

DRYLAND'S END

Set five thousand years in the future, *Dryland's End* takes place in a fabulous techno-empire ruled by intelligent, powerful women. While the Matriarchy has ruled for over two thousand years, and altered human language, thought and society, it is now unraveling. Military rivalries, religious fanaticism and economic competition threaten to destroy the empire from within—just as a rebellion also threatens human existence throughout the galaxy. $12.95/279-5

EDITED BY RANDY TUROFF

LESBIAN WORDS: State of the Art

One of the widest assortments of lesbian nonfiction writing in one revealing volume. Dorothy Allison, Jewelle Gomez, Judy Grahn, Eileen Myles, Robin Podolsky and many others are represented by some of their best work, looking at not only the current fashionability the media has brought to the lesbian "image," but important considerations of the lesbian past via historical inquiry and personal recollections. A fascinating, provocative volume, *Lesbian Words* is a virtual primer to contemporary trends in lesbian thought. $10.95/340-6

MICHAEL ROWE

WRITING BELOW THE BELT: Conversations with Erotic Authors

Journalist Michael Rowe interviewed the best erotic writers—both those well-known for their work in the field and those just starting out—and presents the collected wisdom in *Writing Below the Belt*. Rowe speaks frankly with cult favorites such as Pat Califia, crossover success stories like John Preston, and up-and-comers Michael Lowenthal and Will Leber. $19.95/363-5

EURYDICE

f/32

"Its wonderful to see a woman...celebrating her body and her sexuality by creating a fabulous and funny tale."

—Kathy Acker

With the story of Ela (whose name is a pseudonym for orgasm), Eurydice won the National Fiction competition sponsored by Fiction Collective Two and Illinois State University. A funny, disturbing quest for unity, *f/32* prompted Frederic Tuten to proclaim "almost any page ... redeems us from the anemic writing and banalities we have endured in the past decade..." $10.95/350-3

LARRY TOWNSEND

ASK LARRY

Starting just before the onslaught of AIDS, Townsend wrote the "Leather Notebook" column for *Drummer* magazine, tackling subjects from sexual technique to safer sex, whips to welts, Daddies to dog collars. Now, readers can avail themselves of Townsend's collected wisdom as well as the author's contemporary commentary—a careful consideration of the way life has changed in the AIDS era. $12.95/289-2

ORDERING IS EASY!

MC/VISA orders can be placed by calling our toll-free number

PHONE 800-375-2356 / FAX 212 986-7355

or mail this coupon to:

MASQUERADE BOOKS
DEPT. W74A, 801 2ND AVE., NY, NY 10017

BUY ANY FOUR BOOKS AND CHOOSE ONE ADDITIONAL BOOK, OF EQUAL OR LESSER VALUE, AS YOUR FREE GIFT.

QTY.	TITLE	NO.	PRICE
			FREE
			FREE

W74A

	SUBTOTAL
	POSTAGE and HANDLING
We Never Sell, Give or Trade Any Customer's Name.	**TOTAL**

In the U.S., please add $1.50 for the first book and 75¢ for each additional book; in Canada, add $2.00 for the first book and $1.25 for each additional book. Foreign countries: add $4.00 for the first book and $2.00 for each additional book. No C.O.D. orders. Please make all checks payable to Masquerade Books. Payable in U.S. currency only. New York state residents add 8¼% sales tax. Please allow 4-6 weeks delivery.

NAME _____

ADDRESS _____

CITY _____ STATE _____ ZIP _____

TEL ( ) _____

PAYMENT: ☐ CHECK ☐ MONEY ORDER ☐ VISA ☐ MC

CARD NO. _____ EXP. DATE _____